MAD
MADDY

DAVID GEARING

AKUSAI
PUBLISHING

ISBN 0692719482

EAN13 978-0692719480

MAD MADDY

1

JAMES

I swear to God I saw her when I was six. Staring into the mirror, I did everything Alanis told me to do. I turned around three times, said her name, "Mad Maddy, Mad Maddy, Mad Maddy," and opened my eyes.

Now Bobby down the street will tell you that her red eyes—a scorching hellfire red—will burn your soul. Her cheeks glow a bright, fiery white. If you believe Bobby, that is. I don't. Not since he lied to his father about the crash that totaled his old Dodge.

But there she was, clawing at the insides of the mirror, like how Mrs. Holloway's Rottweiler always tried to do, trying to eat my throat. Her hair fell from her face, covering all but her glowing red-orange eyes, burning like candles in the dark. Her hands—more claws than fingers—scraped and tore at me. Her mouth gaped open in a wild dog snarl.

That night I learned that you really can believe everything you hear. I also learned that an extra pair of underwear is always a good idea.

I'm not expecting you to believe me. Shit, I'm not even sure I believe me when I tell the story.

When I close my eyes—even blink when I retell it—my back cries out in pain, my eyes feel blinded by the pale skin and her flaming irises.

I feel it all over again.

My heart knows it happened. My brain says it's all bullshit.

I got so scared of her that I fell backward into the wall. When I crashed back, I damn near took down the towel rack, that pathetic aluminum foil bar that my dad half-assed screwed into the wall to keep my mother quiet. I sure wish he did a better job screwing that thing in, cuz it fell backward and scraped up my back as I slid down.

Much more afraid than hurt, I cried like it ripped right into me three inches deep.

That's when my mom comes bursting into the bathroom, flicking on the light and there wasn't a damn thing to be seen nowheres. Mad Maddy just disappeared into the mirror world, or the grave, or wherever the fuck she'd come from.

I started laughing. How could I not laugh? Three seconds before that, I was nearly screaming my head off at some scary bitch behind the mirror.

Then, my mom walks in and there I am, still screaming my head off while my mom freaks out about me waking her up and she's gotta get to work early the next day.

I laughed so hard Mom had to drag me out of the bathroom by my hands and wrists. My swimming trunks nearly yanked off my bottom, she was pulling me so hard.

And yes, if you want to ask, I'll tell you. I still laugh at everything that scares me. It's my natural reaction to laugh it all off.

Most people consider me some sort of sicko, laughing at halls of mirrors, in bathrooms, in rich people's houses.

When I get a new car, the first thing I do is take off all the mirrors. The inside rearview. The outside side-view mirrors, I paint over with a chalk spray from do-it-yourself stores. Covers the glass and keeps her inside.

If the eyes are the windows to your soul, mirrors are the windows to your nightmares.

It's this that runs through my head when I clean out my grandfather's attic three months after he was placed in long-term care.

"No, I'm not going," I tell my mom. "I can't step inside of that house."

An exasperated sigh blows into my ear from seven miles of telephone wire. "James, don't go through this again. I'm going to need your help. Pop Pop had too much stuff for me to rummage alone."

"Get dad to help you out. Neighbors? Anyone?"

My mom pauses, a sudden drop in her tone. "James Preston." She pauses, sighs again. "Listen, honey," she says. "I know that it's hard for you to do this, believe me. It's hard for me, too."

My brain listens to her reasons. She needs an extra hand. My dad's not available—out of town for work. My neighbors don't need to be going through my family's precious stuff. They all sound sincere, and I want to believe her.

But my heart pulses fear and adrenaline, like sonar, searching for the obstacles and traps.

"Fine, I'll go," I say. I'm only half joking when I say, "Did Pop Pop get rid of all the mirrors in his living room?"

Mom meets me in the driveway. Her eyes look heavy as sandbags, begging for sleep. With her arms folded across her chest in exaggerated disappointment, I start to think that I shouldn't have slept in that extra half hour.

"Took you long enough," she says. She checks her phone, raises her eyes up to meet mine. "You didn't answer my text."

"I was trying to get here as fast as possible." My eyes turn downward to avoid the disappointment in hers. "Sorry, mom."

I wait for her to acknowledge my apology only to watch her let herself into the house. The screen door goes tha-whap like an exclamation mark at the end of an argument.

I don't like admitting that I haven't been to this house in nearly five years. You see, my Pop Pop had an old décor in his house, a classical décor that he refused to touch. Maw Maw decorated it when they had moved in. Spent a great deal of money on it, too.

The vases on the pedestals near the entrance to the house are all real vases from old, expensive cultures. The crystal cabinet with the mirrored background that showcased all of the angel ornaments and collectors' statues of angels holding babies that she had collected over the years in the form of Christmas presents and birthday gifts.

On one wall in every room hangs a mirror. Large mirrors. Some article in some decorating housewife magazine told her that mirrors open up a room, gives the illusion that it's much bigger than it really was.

A large room? That was my Maw Maw's dream.

She had come from money, and lots of it. The kind of money that doesn't think twice about going on vacation and redecorates a house from carpet to ceiling at least once a year. Twice a year if the antidepressant medication ran out.

My Maw Maw's latest phase was mirrors. Elegant the way you think of English royalty elegant. The way intricately carved gold frames and marble pedestals and velvet everything is some kind of rich you only see in high-end furniture stores.

Needless to say, there wasn't anything you could do to get me in that house when I was younger.

When I was ages ten to twelve, I mysteriously had the flu every year around Christmas. When I turned fifteen, I had migraines. At seventeen, I had allergies.

The last time I saw my grandmother, I couldn't wait to open my seventh birthday present. Maw Maw always had the best presents and found the best, warmest sweaters.

Well, for everybody else.

What I got instead was a mess of socks and underwear. My sister? She got money and a promise of a shopping spree.

I knew where I stood.

And where I stood? I stood at the entrance of the house, a grandfather clock staring me right in the face. The shiny golden pendulum swung back and forth, counting the seconds that I stood motionless.

If you have to know, no, I wasn't afraid. I was just resting is all. It was a long drive all the way here.

"Mom?" I shout. "I'll be in the attic." Mirrors, there will be less of them in there. I can be safe.

With closed eyes, I march from one step to the next. The narrow steps take much concentration with your eyes open, let alone closed.

Step by step I listen to each step creak.

God, how I don't miss any of that.

After three creaks, I figure "fuck it" and just run up the steps.

The old steps scream from old age, my abuse fueled by fear. The narrow hallway, the low ceiling above, the creaking steps. If this wasn't my grandparents' house, I'd say I was on a Hollywood set for an Exorcist wannabe remake.

At the top of the steps, three more bedrooms at the end of the hall. Each one lies with doors closed.

In my mind, I wonder which one had my dead grandmother in it. The image of her lying still, hand folded across her chest, the other hanging off the bed and swinging back and forth, it runs back and forth on my mind. A film on replay.

I close my eyes and start humming a song to myself. "Nothing's gonna hurt you, the way the words do."

"James?" my mother calls out to me. "Are you in the attic yet?"

A burst of air escapes my lips. "No, Mom, I just got up here." Like the scared ingrate that I am, I roll my eyes and take a deep breath. "I'll be down there as soon as I can."

Silence from the downstairs tells me that my mother decided that's a good enough answer.

The doors, the thin ones, they can stay closed. Mom didn't need that stuff anyway, I don't think.

I look upwards, a red and white-striped elastic rope remains tied snug against hook in the ceiling. I remember Pop Pop winding and unwinding that rope nearly every summer I'd come and visit. When I was little, it was always fun to imagine the great stuff up there.

To this day, I still can't watch those movies where people discover great treasures—lamps, necklaces, photo albums—without thinking about those times my Pop Pop would leave me by the stairs. With a thick knuckle, white hairs protruding from his fingers, he'd point at me and whisper to keep quiet.

When he came down to see us, he always had a neat new jacket from World War II. A French uniform from World War I. Pins and metal toy airplanes. Imagine the treasures up there.

I lick my lips, taking a gasp of air and tug on the rope. The red plastic ball at the end nearly knocks me on the head, then brings the rest of the ceiling with it.

A ladder comes down. So dusty, it's gray, not brown. It extends down to the floor and the dark empty mouth of the attic awaits.

Oh, to be six again.

My left hand grasps the ladder and I take a deep breath. The wood feels surprisingly sturdy, and I realize I have no idea just how old this house really is. No one ever told me, and that old story about how your grandparents build their house after the war?

Well, we never had that story.

These thoughts leave my mind, flutter by like insects as I climb hand-hand, foot-foot up the ladder.

The darkness gives way to a few stray beams of light that invade from holes in the roof. The holes are dark, frayed near the edges. Rain or birds, I can't tell.

I ain't never had a house problem to deal with. That's the beauty of having an office manager at an apartment complex.

"James?"

"What, Mom?"

"How is it up there?"

"It's fine, Mom."

"Need me to come up?"

"No, I'm good. I just need to get my bearings so I know what I'm looking at." I take a breath and look at the boxes and crates. "Is there anything I should be keeping an eye out for?"

My mother's momentary silence ends with the phrase, "Photos?"

"Alrighty then."

My mother's footsteps trail away downstairs and I let out a breath. Anxiety squeezes my chest, grabbing my lungs in its angry, tight fists. Count down from ten.

Nine.

Eight.

My breathing slows, my hands don't feel so sweaty and tight.

Seven. My eyes trace the sides of the floor. At points, it seems to drop off into the itchy insulation below.

Six.

Five.

The fear of falling off into the pink fluff, even though I'm nowhere even near the edge takes my mind.

Four.

Three.

Slow breathing.

Two.

Slow.

One.

The size of the ceiling belies the size of this attic. I mean, I would have had no idea that it extended this far behind me, either. Talk about resourceful.

Without a clear direction of what to do, I follow the trail of light to a stack of boxes, the flaps folded into each other into a pinwheel shape.

2

JAMES

"Are you ready for lunch? I made tuna sandwiches."

The tangy smell of fresh tuna fish sandwiches would beat out the dusty mold that's probably giving me some kinda nervous disorder or some kind of disease. That's for damned sure. But the faster this gets done, the better.

"No, Mom, I'm good for now." This next box has nothing written on the outsides, just like everything else. "I'll come down in a little bit. How is that?"

My mother mumbles something. I can only guess I've pissed her off again. There's nothing to really say except "Sorry."

I mean, she got me out here. What else does she want?

A quick look over the boxes reveals more clothes shoved away for the winter. My Maw Maw's plan seemed to be store warmer winter clothes in the attic until October, replace with summer clothing. In March, replace winter clothes, take out summer.

These boxes have been here for a few months, to say the least. The layers of dust are at least three times what I have at my apartment.

Either Maw Maw was a slob or she couldn't get up here.

My heart stops, chest squeezes.

My grandmother couldn't reach this area on her own, and I wonder how many months she spent cold, huddled in blankets before someone helped her to jackets and coats during the winter.

"Mom?" I call out. I listen to apparently no one to call me back. "Never mind," I mutter. Apparently to myself.

I close the box, flap over flap like it was before, and push it off to the side. It glides over the dust and wood real easy.

Then, my heart moves, jumps in my chest. "Shit!" I scream out, pushing myself backward into a support beam. "Rats?" I scream. "Rats!"

My mother doesn't reply from downstairs. Must be busy with something else. She'll be sorry when she finds her son dead, eaten to death by a rat.

As my eyes refocus on the movement, I realize nothing has moved. An airy giggle leaves my lips. "You're kidding me," I say.

Where I thought I saw a rat wasn't a rat. Not a mouse or rodent. No birds.

A box, black as our old dog, Sandy, protrudes from the hole left from moving the box. The outsides of it remained clean, free of dust.

"Mom?" I say, but barely loud enough for anyone to really hear me.

My hands grasp the box and tug it from behind the boxes. No one has labeled this one either, and I begin to wonder just how lazy everyone was. Either Pop Pop didn't want to label everything, or he didn't want anyone to find this box.

All the better reason to rummage through it.

My fingertips trace the edge of the box, looking for the lid. Most of it feels smooth, except for a metal ridge in the back. A hinge. My fingers find the crevice between the box and the lid and trace it to the front of the box. The black of the box was so deep, I couldn't even see the hint of separation. The texture feels smooth, black velvet, but so soft I could be running my hands in bath water. No light shines off the metal hinges.

"Which war did you get this from, Pop Pop?"

My hands grab the sides of the lid and pull up. It gives resistance at first, then finally gives in to my demand.

The box opens up without any noise, fresh as the day it was first made.

Inside, a deep red, maroon cloth covering the contents. I tug at the cloth. It, too, feels warm and soft, almost silky, but smoother.

"Wow, Pop Pop, spare no expense."

The cloth flutters off the box, revealing a silver picture frame. The frame is simple, a solid silver bar joined into a five-by-eight border.

The picture reveals a woman. A woman with—

No.

My reaction throws the picture off into the distance, down the hatch to the hallway downstairs.

Fuck!

My shoulders and lungs, they hurt. Like my heart is pulling everything into my chest. My reaction is to grab my chest, my neck, then pound my chest as I'm struggling to breathe.

Everything feels fuzzy in my lungs. Dust covers my tongue with every gasp. My lips form the words, "Mom," but all I can do is gasp for air.

Get out.

Have to get out.

The light from the hallway calls my name as I climb, pulling myself, to the ladder. My first leg, shaky and unsure, finds a ladder rung and stays still long enough for me to slide down the ladder and hit the floor.

Where my face lies, three inches in front of me is her. Smiling.

"Mom!" I scream and slam my eyes shut. My forearms guard my face. Pull my legs in, my body's reaction is to protect myself. "She's going to get me. She's going to get me again!"

"What the hell is wrong with you?" My mother stands above me holding a royal blue ceramic plate in her hands. "Your sandwich is going to spoil, James. Are you going to eat it or not?"

My caring mother that she is, Mom pulls my hand to grab my attention and then holds the plate in front of me.

"Want one?"

"Who the hell is that?" I say.

"You look like you've seen a god damned ghost, James." She lowers the plate in front of me, then rests it down in front between my legs. "I made it your favorite, with Kosher pickles."

"Mom!" I shout. "Who is that?" I throw my hands at the picture without really looking at it. I can't meet her eyes.

"This?" Mom says. She picks up the picture and caresses the glass with her hands. Mom wipes the dust off onto her pants leg and smiles. "That's Marilee."

"Why does Pop Pop have pictures of Mad Maddy?"

My mother looks at me and winces. "You're back on that?" she says. "I think we took you off the medications too early."

Those baby blue pills that were supposed to help with my anxiety. I stopped taking them when I was eight.

The conversation was a difficult one, more so with my parents than for me.

"You don't need those pills," they said. "You need to live without it. Learn coping mechanisms."

"But, I like them. I need them." My little hands held the bottle of pills behind me, daring them to come and pry them out of my little sausage fingers.

"See that?" Mom said. "You're addicted."

She took the pills and put them in a cabinet in her bathroom.

I never saw them again, and two interesting things started that day. My mother began to behave much calmer than before, almost sleepy. Sedate.

I had to keep going to appointments with my doctor, where he would ask me about my fears, my worries, how I handled stress. When he asked if I was feeling stressed out, my mother nodded from behind the doctor. Her mouths forming the words, "Say yes."

The loyal and obedient son that I was, I said, "Yes, sir."

After the appointment, my mother dropped me off with my father and went to pick up a few things from the store. My father sighed at the sight of me.

"Did you have another appointment?" he asked.

I nodded.

He sighed and went to the refrigerator for another drink.

The other thing that started that day? I began my first record streak of being awake: thirty-two hours straight.

Mom takes the plate and carries it down the stairs, negotiating them with less effort than it ever took for me.

"Mom, don't run from me. Who is Marilee?"

"She was a family friend. Your Pop Pop called her his girlfriend, but no one really took him seriously."

"Girlfriend?" My neck struggles to finish the sentence with the sour lump lagging behind the words.

"Yeah, but you remember your Pop Pop. He always had girlfriends around town."

"I always figured we were joking."

"So did your Maw Maw."

I pause, raising an eye.

"How do you know who she is?"

"Eat your sandwich, hun."

"Mom?"

My mother picks up a piece of the sandwich and holds it near my mouth. It waves back and forth in view of my eyes.

I open my mouth and the airplane lands on my tongue.

If I showed you where I live, you'd think I was hiding.

My apartment could best be described as "bat cave minimalist." Black sheets hang from the insides of the walls. I taped tin foil over the windows to make sure that no other light escapes into the windows.

The apartment complex doesn't ask questions, and they're usually nice enough to give me a few days' notice before coming in and looking around. Apparently that's legal for, you know, whatever they want.

I tell them that I have a skin condition. I'm photo-sensitive. I need darkness or it interrupts the melanin in my skin. For the most part, they buy it.

It's not that I'm a vampire. I love sunlight. I really do.

But any light leads to reflection, which leads to panic attacks and nightmares. This leads to hospitalization and a three thousand dollar emergency room visit for a few pills and a good night's sleep.

My mother, she refuses to come over anymore. She tried that once, back in November shortly after I moved into the apartment. I went to work and so did she. While I was at the bar, my mother rearranged my furniture, gave me really nice, somewhat expensive vertical blinds. She tore down my foil and blankets and made sure to dust.

I came home, dropped my backpack by my feet and ran to close the blinds.

"Have you lost your mind?" I screamed at my mother, the last time I will ever do so in my life.

"I didn't want you to live in a den, James. What is wrong with you? It's so," her face twisted into something of a pretzel, "so dreary. You needed to lighten up a little bit."

My mother rested her hands on the hips of her pants suit. "It really does look so much better."

That night I deliberately picked a fight so I could convince her to go home early. I told her that her roast was dry, the vegetables were inedible and the cinnamon buns she made were too salty.

My mother packed up her things in a quiet, thunder storming mood, then called a cab. I never even had the chance to tell her goodbye and, you know, have a safe trip.

My father called me the next day. "Thanks for ruining my vacation," he said.

"Eat up." My mother rests another sandwich on the blue plate in front of me.

My hands push the plate around the table. As light creeps in from the window in front of me, my eyes stare into the shadows, cast from the vase onto the tablecloth.

"Mom, can you, um, shut those drapes, please?"

My mother looks at me, shrugs and does nothing.

"Mom, seriously?" Just to be on the safe side, I pull the plate into the shadows, keeping the light from reflecting off its own glazed, silvery surface. For sake of argument, I just stand up and close the damned shades myself.

"What is your problem?" Mom says. She opens the shades again and gives me her "don't you dare" stare that she used to give me before I did something stupid.

"Mom, please! The light. It's blinding my eyes." My hands reach out to close the shades, but she slaps my hand. "James Preston, you sit down this instant!" My mother presses her hand on my wrists and looks at my hands. "What has gotten into you?"

I slide the plate off the table.

"Whoops."

I stand up, grab my orange juice off the table and toss it—literally—into the sink. The glass shatters, but I'd barely know it over my mom's scream of frustration and horror.

"James!' she screams after me. "James!"

The screen door thwaps closed behind me.

The sidewalks seem a safer bet. No windows. No mirrors. No reflective car surfaces. I can't drive. No buses.

No windows on the nearest bar, so I decide that I need a drink. A big one.

My eyes take a few seconds to adjust to the smoky, wood interior of the bar. Soft rock plays in the background, giving the pool players something to sing along to. No one else sits at the bar. If there are drunkards left in this town, they haven't even gotten out of bed yet.

"What can I get ya?" the bartender says. His white beard hangs in a stiff point below his chin, held tight with a black rubber band.

"A beer. Please."

"Kind?"

"Something dark. In a dark glass, please. Maybe a mug."

The bartender gives me a look that says that I'm crazy, but not as crazy as the rest of his usual clientele. "I ain't never heard of no one drinking a beer out of a mug," he says.

"Non-reflective?"

The bartender turns around, spinning on his heels, and grabs a glass from the counter behind him.

"Too reflective," I nod. "That one?"

"You'll take the glass I give you, son," he says. The beer fills only halfway with actual liquid, the rest of it all foam.

"Too much head," I say.

The bartender nods his head and laughs. "I wish." He takes a step to the side to help someone at the end of the bar—one of the pool guys asks for more quarters—and I take a sip of the beer.

There, in front of me. There she is. Laughing. Looking. Poking at the glass.

My legs shake, feel weak as I push myself down the side of the bar. I can't walk, my legs won't let me.

I hobble to the left, away. Away. Away.

"That's four bucks, son."

My hands fumble through my pockets, finger counting a number of coins and bills. I don't know what the bills are, but I offer them all to the bartender.

"No, you come over here," he says. His hands wave me in his direction.

"Here you go," I say. The stack of bills and coins—I don't bother to count—jingles a muffled echo into the smoky air.

"No, that means you bring it over here, fucko," he says. His fingers point to the floor, the way my mom used to do.

I'm beginning to realize that I was in trouble way too much.

I hold my ground. My fingers shake, but manage to shove the stack of cash in the bartender's direction.

"What the hell is this?" he says. "Don't half-ass it. Get it over here, or get the hell out of my bar."

I push the stack three inches further, hyper-extending my shoulders as far as I can.

"Maybe you didn't hear me." The bartender smiles, but doesn't smile. He takes heavy, threatening steps to take the money from me, but as he approaches near, it becomes clear that he does not see what I see.

A finger comes from the glass, tapping. A long, dark red fingernail—fire red—taps on the glass. A pair of thick, seductive lips smile from the mirror, but no face. Just lips.

Fuck.

"Sir, you have, um, something."

"Speak up, faggot." The bartender grabs the cash, but his hand stays in a fist, a threatening fist on the dark cherry wood counter. "I don't think I heard you apologize for makin' me walk all the way over here."

"There is something behind you," I say. My tongue forces each syllable out of my mouth like a bulldozer pushing dirt.

"Nice try, asshole, but I've already heard that one before." The bartender grabs the cash and shoves it in the register drawer.

When he lifts his empty fist at me, my first reaction is to flinch. My hands come up over my eyes.

"No, stop!" My hands pry from my face, push the air in front of me away. "She's going to get you!"

My legs give out from underneath me, and for once, I'm thankful. The desk impacts my chin, slamming my head upwards. A shock of pain soars through my jaw to my eyes.

Even my damned nostrils hurt.

"Get him out of here!" the bartender screams. Hands grab my shoulders and my shirt.

"No! Stop!"

My feet hit the tables and chairs. I pull my feet up, stiffen the muscles to maybe catch something and keep from being tugged away.

"You don't understand," I yell. My throat gurgles spit and phlegm. My mouth dry. "She's going to kill all of you."

In the mirror behind the man, a face smiles, then disappears, fading into the reflections of bottles on the shelf.

"You're fucking crazy," I scream. "She'll kill you."

The smile, it gets darker. Darker while smiling at me.

My eyes can't shift away from those lips. I don't see the bartender. I don't see the chairs and table legs that caused me bruise after bruise.

I don't see the whatever it was that trips over me on my way out.

The last thing before the sunlight blinds my sight, are two pairs of dark, blood red lips speaking to me, whispering, "Goodbye, James. Goodbye."

3

JAMES

To travel with my kind of phobia, catoptrophobia, requires a lot of planning and preparation. Failing to plan is planning to fail.

What I suffer from is a fear of reflective surfaces, mirrors, and reflections. This is the technical term my doctor assigned to me when I had to stop working in an office or any retail building.

Catoptrophobia isn't really the right diagnosis, though. Consider a person who has a fear of falling. He's not really afraid of falling. He's afraid of suddenly not falling.

I'm not afraid of reflective surfaces. I'm afraid of them suddenly not being reflective. Maybe having something inside, a girl or a young woman digging her way out to eat your face.

Because of this, when traveling, window seats in airplanes are a no-no. Traveling in a car is a bad idea.

Going into most public places—mostly malls and stores—scare the living hell out of me. It seems that those stores love windows.

With the best of intentions, I can walk to the mall just down the block from my apartment complex and enter the buildings, but only if I run.

Sometimes, in case you were wondering, the doors don't open fast enough. While they do account for someone walking into the building, they can't open fast enough for a runner.

I've left a few snot trails on glass doors thanks to not knowing that little piece of advice. Another tip for getting into buildings without looking at windows?

It seems contradictory, but glasses.

Use glasses, focus on just one thing and one thing only. Take big steps, enter with a purpose, with a stride that screams power.

For Heaven's sakes, don't actually scream. You just get asked to leave by two very stern security guards.

Not scream, forceful walking. This is what I do when I walk up to the bus station and request a ticket for Saraday, South Carolina.

The woman from behind the counter, she looks at me, blinks twice before she says anything.

"Going where, sir?" Her blank stare, I start to think that maybe it's not for me, maybe for someone else behind me.

Was I speaking some other language?

"Saraday. In South Carolina."

"The closest we can get you is to Columbia," she says. Her black, shiny eyes squint as she reads the computer monitor.

"That could work," I say. "But what about the bus station just outside of the town?"

"We don't have a station out of town," she says. Her voice goes monotone, stale.

"I'm sorry," I say. "I must have remembered something else."

Out of annoyance, I glance around, looking at the posters on the walls. Buses and happy people riding in windows and waving goodbye or hello to happy people on the corner of the street.

Those unsuspecting idiots in the pictures look happy because they don't know what lurks in the world of mirrors. Any time now, these things become imminent dangers.

If our eyes are the windows to our soul, windows are the doors to Hell.

"We can try that," she says. "So will Columbia be it?" she says.

Before I can answer, she extends an open palm, her fake maroon nails all pointing at my chest. "Can I have your ID, sir?"

Hours later, I'm sitting on the bus, not the window aisle, looking at the side of the other seats. The colorful, swirly pattern or oranges and reds on the cloth seats draws me in, a nice contrast to staring at a reflective window all day. Light comes in and blinds my eyes, burning my sight.

But I didn't bring sunglasses.

I can't be blind. I need to see, to be prepared in case she shows up.

Survival of the fittest means survival of the seeing.

It's when I think this and let a breath into a steady, focused stream in front of me, a man climbs into the bus with a wire-haired black dog on a thick, leather handle. The man's glasses are tar black, thick lenses that hide all but the lower half of his face. He smiles. A calm, disarming smile that finds me smiling back at him. And though he looks at me, he never looks at me in the face.

The black lab wears a sign, blue cloth with white lettering that warns everyone not to pet him since he's working.

The man sits next to me, but across the aisle. The dog lies at the man's feet, curled up with his nose pointed in the direction of the aisle.

"Welcome," I say, loud.

The man looks around, seemingly startled from my rather loud introduction.

"I'm over here," I say. My hands wave in front of his face, pointing over at me. I drop them to my lap when my common sense kicks back into high gear.

"I'm blind, sir," he says. "Not deaf."

And yes, I know he can't see it, but I nod anyway. "I'm sorry, sir. I'm a bit nervous."

"I'm just an old man," he says. He extends his hand out to shake mine. "My name is Ronald."

"I'm not nervous about meeting you," I say.

The man, though blind and old, shakes my hand with the force of the jaws of life. Three firm pumps up and down and he releases it.

"You must work out," I say. I shake my hand in the air, letting my fingers slap against my palm to loosen it up.

"Not with my osteoporosis," he says. Ronald smirks.

"I'll just be quiet now. Enough of making an ass out of myself."

Ronald laughs and pats the dog's ears.

"What's his name?" I ask. "Where are you going?"

"We're heading the Charleston," he says. "And my friend here is Spike."

"Well, hello, Spike."

I reach down to pat him on the nose, but the man's voice scares my hand back onto my lap.

"Please don't do that," he says.

"Right. He's working. Sorry."

As I study the man's face and his lack of facial expressions, my glance wanders past his ears to the setting sun in the horizon. The way the light comes through, a brief glimmer of color catches my eye and I blink.

"Is there something wrong?" Ronald asks.

My hands grab my chest. I feel my pulse throb-throbbing through my ribs. "No, no. I'm fine."

"You jumped a little bit," he says. "I heard you gasp."

"It's nothing."

And there, in the mirror behind him, is a woman, fire-red eyes, scratching on the other side of the mirror. Her transparent image scratches at the inside surface of the mirror.

"She's not real," I mutter under my breath. "She's not real."

"Who's not real?" the man asks.

My voice quivers. "Not real?" Fake laugh, let him believe that I'm awkward nervous. "I said surreal." I smile, hoping he can hear it in his voice. "I can't believe I'm going back home."

The old man nods, smiles. "I know what you mean. My grandson gets out of basic training for the army today. I'm going to meet him when he gets home." His head leans backward, slightly looking up. With his glasses on, I can only assume he's trying to take a nap.

Maddy's mirror image scrapes at the inside of the window, floating there without feet or an apparent body. Just head and hands, her green, toothy grin and darkened lips smile. She licks them and her eyes widen.

A fingernail etches a wavy line into the window. A line that apparently no one else can see.

"Um, miss?" I say.

A woman down the aisle shoves a backpack into the seat beside her. She ignores my calls.

"Ma'am? Would you mind trading seats with me?" I say.

Still nothing.

Again, am I speaking a different language?

If I want shit to get done, I have to do it myself.

I say nothing in return. Instead, I grab my bags and move to the back of the bus.

The dog's eyebrows point in my direction, his eyes watching me go down the aisle to the last seat in the middle of the bus. From this angle, I have perfect visibility of the front door, all windows.

My ear buds fit snug into my ear canals and I press play on the mp3 player. I close my eyes, bury my head in a pillow, and let the man's relaxing voice fool me into self-therapy through hypnosis.

Apparently though it's against the rules, we stop at a rest stop on the side of the road. I overhear someone say something about Interstate 20. The dark nighttime sky looks etched with clouds, lit with bright halos by the moon from behind.

The herbal smell of wet, green grass gives me a good reason to take a deep breath and enjoy the freedom of surroundings. Only dark wooden buildings surround us. Not a single other vehicle in sight. A line of elderly folks takes up both bathrooms.

True to the power of suggestion, it's not until I see everyone waddling, pacing back and forth, and doing the potty dance that I realize I gotta piss, too.

The blind man is, I don't know where. His dog is probably pooping, too. The perks of being blind is, you don't have to pick up your own poop.

More perks of being blind? You never realize that they are out to get you. The signs just pass you by.

We should all be so lucky.

The line moves slow as two men strike up a conversation about a television. The man holds his hands up, squares out his arms and says, "The new one I got is plasma. About this big. I had to have it delivered it was so big."

The other adjusts his shirt sleeves, pulling them up his liver-spotted forearms, thick, dark strands of hair forming a sleeve up to his wrists. "Yeah, mine is fifty-four inches."

This must be the new rulers. When you can't compare penis sizes, you compare cars and televisions.

"Have you seen the new organic plasma flatscreens?" I butt in. "Now if you want to see nice screens, you should see yourself one of those." Both men drop their guards, turn to see me. "We're talking beautiful, laser crisp images. Ten-eighty dpi, a refresh rate that makes it look like it's happening in your living room. Whatever you watch."

The men, one of them still wearing a Member's Only jacket after all these decades, their jaws drop open. Member's Only says, "I saw one of those." His voice carries bass like a drum, but throaty with a Brooklyn twist. He points a big-knuckled pointer finger at his buddy in line. "I nearly got one, but it was too big to carry."

"Why not just have it delivered, eh?"

"They said they were out of them," the man says. He shrugs, looks at me, checking to see if I'm impressed.

I smile and shrug.

"See?" the man says, points at me, his yellow fingernail only centimeters from my face. "He knows. He knows."

We follow the line until finally, a bright silver—and very wet—stall waits for me to finally piss. The toilet, the buttons, everything is a chrome, brushed silver that is more scratched and etched than brushed. My hands grip my pants button, then switch to my zipper.

For a few seconds. I can hold it. Maybe just pee. I don't really need to shit.

My finger grabs my zipper and pulls it down. With a careful

finger, I reach into my fly, through my boxers. Like fishing in the dark, my hands have a hard time grabbing my dick, so flaccid and scared I can barely find it. My eyes remained affixed on the metal of the toilet. Every reflective surface gets a good once or twice over, keeping the whole area in check.

"Please, God, please not here," I mumble. Apparently loud enough for someone else to hear because Member's Only jacket knocks on the door.

"You okay in there?" he asks.

I wave him off, bang back on the door. His feet squeak in the sticky, piss-wet floor on the way out. "Leave me be," I scream.

Deep breaths. Pause, count to five, slowly. One. Two.

Grab my button and undo it, the top of my pants hang loose from my hips. I thank God I have an ass, it being the only thing that keeps my pants from falling to the ground.

Take a deep breath, James. Take a breath. Let it out slow.

As the air leaves my lips, I pull down the waistband of my boxers and let my dick hang.

Grab hold, aim.

Fire in a slow, steady stream.

If I'm scared to death, the last thing I need to do is let a stream of freaked out, uncontrollable piss all over my pants.

Yes, I've thought about this stuff.

I can't look down, so I piss blind. All I can do is listen for a steady splash into the bowl. So far, so good. My bladder empties, and it's amazing what a few seconds of pee can do for you.

My entire body feels less tense. A headache I didn't even know I had from holding it all in, it fades into the blackness of my mind.

Even my own asshole unclenches.

At the end of the last few drips, a nagging feeling to look down, watch and make sure that I made it all into the toilet.

Yes, it's a public toilet. Yes, other people haven't bothered to check. Why should I care?

Creature of habit, I guess.

When I do look down, it's only for a second before I thrust my head upwards, peek at the ceiling, looking at the wide, scratched-at holes. The dark brown stains, getting darker and browner. The nagging image of someone literally flinging poo at the ceiling to get those stains.

It takes all kinds.

I shake once, twice, then tuck everything back in. The emptiness of the restroom suggests that I might want to hurry up. There's no guarantee that the driver will even notice me, let alone wait for me to finish.

Maybe one of the old guys will say something. Maybe.

Take no chances. Grab my pants, button them up and hurry outside.

But, I must wash my hands.

I listen, paused and holding my breath. My heart, the only thing that is making any noise whatsoever.

You know the routine, James. Close your eyes, reach in front of you. Turn the knob. Lift the handle. See which makes water come out.

Stick hands under water, rub around. Soap, lather. Rinse. Don't bother repeating because it'll kill you.

My wet hands slap damp paint, then grasp, almost clawing, to the right of me. My hands wander to the left, then to the right. No sign of a paper towel dispenser. No air dryer for your hands.

It's panic and fear that forces my eyes wide open.

Don't turn your head, James. Don't look in the mirror.

My hands grab for the giant plastic box hanging off the wall. Press the gray lever downward and wait for the brown towel to come on out.

From the corner of my eye, a movement, a shadow flickers in the light.

It's the light above, the fluorescent light. There's a reason why these things are in horror movies. Ol' Unreliable. Every light in every bathroom everywhere. Every time.

Take a breath and face my fears. My psychologist says it's important to do this. Confront them little by little when I'm ready.

I ask myself, "Am I ready?"

"Hey, you ready in there?" Members Only says from a crack in the door.

I nod. "Yes."

The shadow flickers again.

I know it's a bad idea to, but I look anyway.

Something itches along the side of my forearm.

I know it's a bad idea, it always is. Scary movies, if nothing else, taught me to not look when some creepy shit goes on.

As I turn to leave, a voice echoes from behind me. "Excuse me," it says. The voice is feminine.

"Who's that you got in there?" the man asks. He adjusts his jacket, pulls up his sleeves. "You got a lady in there?" His face beams while his eyes try to keep peeking over my shoulder.

"No, it's nothing," I say. My hand pushes him in the direction of the bus. "Let's get going."

The door tries to close behind me, but never makes a noise, never closes completely.

My heart thunders in my chest so hard it rattles my shoulders. Don't look. Don't look.

True to the idiot that I am, I turn anyway. Peek through the sides of my eyes, peripheral vision. I see nothing, not even a quick glance into the mirror on the other side of the bathroom.

A sigh escapes. "Nothing," I say. "Good."

"Nothing?" the man says. For a minute, I forget he is there.

I shake my head, wave him away. "Let's go."

But I don't. I can't. My pants won't move. I kick, pull, then jerk my foot forward.

Whatever you do, James, don't look back.

"Let the fuck go," I say.

Member's Only looks at me, turns his head to the side. "What's taking you so long? C'mon."

"Just a minute," I say. I kick, pull, tug.

Nothing.

God dammit. Take a gulp. Remember to do this quickly. Just a second, look down.

My breath picks up. My chest tightens and gasps for quick, thin bursts of oxygen. Calm. Down.

Just calm the fuck down.

Okay.

Ready?

One peek down, and something rubs against my ankle.

I can't do this. My eyes look upwards, snapping from left to right. White and brown stains fills my sight, but anything is better than this.

I tug my foot forward.

"Let! Go!" I say.

I snap my foot forward and instead of a gentle rub against my ankle, something scratches.

Sweat itches down my back, my shoulders grasp tighter to my bones.

"Fuck, fuck. Fuck."

Members Only comes to the door of the bathroom and rests his hand on mine, now grasping the side of the doorway. "You coming or not?" he asks. "I can't get him to wait all damn night."

"My foot is caught in the door," I say. My eyes motion downward, but never connect with the ground.

Try as I might, my mouth won't move beyond that. No syllables let me tell him that he's walking into a trap. That we both might die that night.

"You're kidding me," he says. "I hate when that happens. Usually happens to me when I've had a little too much, you know what I'm saying?" he says. Then he pauses. Members Only peers into my eyes with a "caught ya" smile.

"I'm not drunk," I whisper.

"You aren't looking too good," he says. "Here, let me take a look."

My pant leg slides along the yellowish-clear liquid on the floor, gliding backward back into the bathroom. Members Only apparently doesn't see a damned thing.

"Can you hurry up?" I say.

He nods. Crouching on his knees, he looks at the door and then my foot. "What the hell is this?" he says.

Something sharp cuts into my right ankle.

Then the meaty slap of hands on the wet floor. Members Only shrieks.

I reverse hiss, breathing in the air to keep from screaming like a girl. Wincing in pain, I grasp for my knee. A stream of blood dilutes in the running

Members Only slaps the sticky piss pond with his hands. He slip-n-slides backward into the waterfall coming from the bathroom stall—the same stall I pissed in.

The cut isn't deep, burns a little, but isn't deep. With the flood of dirty truck stop bathroom water and my own urine, Members Only can only be swimming toward death.

"Hey!" What's his name? Robert? Roger? Lenny? "Are you okay?"

Water splashes, gurgles.

Take a deep breath. "Help! Somebody! Help!"

My eyes. Keep looking forward. Don't look back. Then she can't get you.

No one comes, no sign of anyone actually hearing me.

He slaps at the ground again. His screams shake the walls of the bathroom. He sounds like he's gargling on spit or blood.

I turn around, take a deep breath to keep from passing out, breathe it all out into slow, steady breaths. Slow. Steady.

Turning around, the stall door shuts in a wall-shaking slam.

And I can't explain why my feet turn against me and bring me to the bathroom stall door. I punch into the door, knocking it back and forth with each of my girly punches. "Don't let her take you!" I scream. The words burn my throat like acidic vomit. "Don't let her take you!"

Slam. Slam. Slam.

Then, the door bounces so hard it unlocks. The lights go out, and deep in my gut, it's her.

"Fuck you, you won't take me, too!"

My feet scatter all over the floor and it's nearly impossible to keep my balance. The coffee smell of my own piss comes back into my nose when I fall, my hands the only thing that keeps my face from bathing in my own waste.

"Fuck you." My fingers grab around at the dirty piss and shit-filled grout. With each grip, my hands pull me closer and closer to the front door.

The fresh breeze of chilly air brushes my face from underneath the bathroom door. The handle of the door helps me to stand up on my own wobbly feet.

I don't bother thinking about the rest. I already know where he is, and who he's with.

God help me, I just can't go back.

I can't.

"I'm sorry," I say.

My foot won't support all of my weight, so I nudge one foot forward and limp to the bus.

"Where's Hank?" the driver says.

I shrug, shake my head quickly without looking him in the eye.

"What the hell does that mean?" he says. He stands on the first step, then the second. His eyes follow me to the back of the bus. "What does that mean? Where is he?"

"I'm not the one who did anything. He just disappeared." For what it's worth, I know I'm not lying.

Yes, I still feel bad about it.

He can see the tears just beneath the surface. I know he can see them because his face softens. His shoulders drop.

The driver's navy blue jacket puffs at the chest pocket. Probably cigarettes. It puffs even further as he moves his hands in front of him, pointing at me. "You. Come up here."

"I didn't do anything." My eyes look straight ahead.

In the nighttime, with the interior lights on, every window on this joint turns into a window, a potential window to Hell.

I point at the door. "Check the bathroom or something. I think I saw him go in there."

The driver nods and waddles off the bus. I follow him as far as the edge of the bus and wait outside. Short, determined steps carry the man to the front of the bathroom and he takes a quick peek inside.

Quick, in this case, means only half a second.

Next, he's hightailing it to the bus. "Let's go," he says.

The other riders gasp, demand answers. "Where is Hank?"they say. "What happened to him? Did he catch a ride? Someone pick him up?"

The scenarios that the other riders tell themselves get more and more creative as time moves on. In one rumor, a hooker picks him up and offers to take him to Las Vegas. The complete opposite direction.

I bite my own tongue and sigh.

The door squeals and unfolds to close.

The other riders, they all peer through the window, shading out the rest of the lighting with their hands to create something like darkened binoculars.

"What happened?" a woman in a yellow bonnet asks the driver.

"It's best if you sit down," he says.

I glance at the rubber floor of the bus, counting the circles that stick out from the base. With a smile, I stop at seventeen and lay my head on my bag. A jacket covers my head. Ignorance is bliss.

He deserved to die. He had to have. Someone had to be sacrificed so that I could live.

But that nagging feeling that she missed, that I somehow dodged a bullet meant for me.

The last thought to travel through my brain is a scream that echoes in the bathroom, a steady babbling stream of pink blood-piss-water combination flooding the bottoms of my shoes.

I yawn, slow my breathing, and rest my eyes.

And try as I might, I can't sleep. My eyelids become like movie theater screens. Images, moving images, of people dying, blood, screams.

All of this caves into my head and forces my eyes open, just to make sure.

I know I'm up against a wall, the metal of the inside of the bus, but I shiver. Feeling my ass muscles clench all the way up to my shoulders, I try to keep the shake the sudden feeling that I'm fucked, that this was all a bad idea, and I'm not able to do anything about it.

"I need to get off," I say. This is less a statement and more of a demand.

"What's that?" an old woman next to me says.

"Off," I say. "Me. Now. Get off."

The woman's face comes together in the center of her face. She's either disgusted or processing, I'm not sure which.

"Please," I say. My hands grip the handles of my bag and I drag it to the front of the bus.

The bus driver's tired, weary eyes lock onto mine and he stops cold in his tracks.

"What's the matter?" he says, nods in my direction.

"I need to get off. This was a bad idea," I say. "Very, very bad idea."

The driver makes the same damned disappointed face that the lady made before him. Yes, I know I'm a disappointment. No, you don't understand.

"Please, can you drop me off at the next station?" I ask.

"There is no station nearby." He shrugs and diverts his eyes back to the road.

"You're fucking serious?" I ask. My knuckles grip the seats on either side of the aisle with such force, my tendons slingshot on either side of my knuckles. "I need to get off." Brief pause. "Somewhere safe, of course."

An exasperated sigh, then, "If I let you off in the next gas station, can you please shut the hell up?"

I nod to shake the feeling of being watched, but the driver takes it as a yes. "Good, now just sit down. You can't be all over the aisles while the bus is moving."

When I sit back down in my seat, I don't have to look up to realize I'm being watched. Each pair of eyes drilling into my head, into my brain, to make sure I feel humiliated.

Already my mom's voice sounds off in my head like a marine drill sergeant. "Have you no shame? I know your momma taught you better than that."

With a soft, velvety wrinkled hand the woman next to me grasps my right knee, barely squeezing. "You want something to help you out?" she asks. Between her index finger and her thumb, she rolls two light yellow pills. "These should help," she says with a smile. "I used to feel motion sickness when I traveled all the time. Now I take these and poof! I'm out!" The way she smiles, her entire face seems to follow her lips backward. Loose, like curtains pulled back to let in the midday sun.

"Thank you," I say and extend my hand. The capsules are big, horse pills, my mom used to say. I don't bother to examine, but shove them into my mouth and swallow.

Mirrors, dangerous, and everything else being reflective this late in the evening, I just stare at the rubber matting of the floor. It reflects the yellow-orange of the street lights outside, passing in lines that remind me of the landing lights on an airstrip.

It took six tries and twelve Prozac to get my driver's license. Let me tell you, it wasn't for a lack of trying.

You know that part where the instructor always tells you, "Fasten your seatbelt and check your mirrors?"

Well, I can't do that part without wanting to shit myself, and it's really hard to shit yourself in private while your instructor waits for you to put your hands on ten and two.

These are the random things I remember while I rent my first car since I was twenty-two. To be fair, I rented the car under my name, but my girlfriend at the time drove.

It's this I think about when I finally drive from Columbia to Saraday in a car that took me nearly three hours to rent. Not because they were busy, but because it takes a lot of Prozac and more mysterious yellow pills to work up the courage to sit in a car, surrounded by your worst nightmares.

During geography, the one thing they never tell you is that South Carolina is a whole lot of nothing. And by nothing, I mean absolutely, jack shit, bullshit nothing.

Metal sign posts telling you not to pass and lots and lots and lots of green. Moss, trees. Green forests and low bridges just three inches off the water.

But that's about it. That's where I find it best to avoid all contact with reflective surfaces and drive as fast as I can within legal limits.

A whole lot of life-blooming green and brown water pass me by as my car carries me further and further away from Columbia.

The sky covers humid subtropical jungle, a smooth baby blue that spreads far into the blurry horizon, a horizon covered by mirage after mirage of oases on the roads.

When I was too young to realize what they were, I used to think that these were really water puddles, drying up before we used to get to them.

My dad drove faster until we finally reached them—or didn't reach them, as the case may be—and I'd spot another one on the horizon, saying, "Daddy! Let's get that one! Hurry!"

Sure enough, he'd slam on the gas and we'd speed toward it like there were no cops around.

In South Carolina, Saraday to be exact, we didn't have many cops. There wasn't reason for them. Well, mostly. We was a small town of blue-collar workers and little kids who liked to ride our bikes until our parents called us in for dinner.

That was nearly thirty years ago.

Today, it's a whole new world, and not in that cute little Disney way.

This small, failing town has turned itself into a huge disaster of Godzilla proportions. Drugs, check cashing places, bars. Everything opened up after mining went under.

Last we heard from my mom's sister, Aunt Marie, one of our principals was kicked out of the school for using drugs in his office.

A car accelerates behind me, the reflection of the sun damn near blinds me. My hands react, pulling off the steering wheel and grasping my eyes, rubbing them until I see red and black dots dance before my eyes.

I turn my head to look behind me and his lights flash. Asshole wants me to move over and let his cherry red Volkswagen to pass through. I thought Volkswagens weren't in a hurry to get anywhere.

It's the middle of the daytime, about four-thirty with the sun high in the sky, baking us all, and this Volkswagen thinks I need to get out of the way.

My hands flashback to the present, seizing the steering wheel as I feel the thud thud thud of the wake-up strips along the side of the road. The car's tires bounce against the ribbed shoulder like a flat tire, which is enough to get me to clench my asshole tight and ignore the jackass behind me.

Damp sweat forms around my neck and I begin counting, trying to remember the white number that told me just how far until the next rest stop.

I count backward, subtracting mile from mile, until my brain rests on the number fourteen.

Fourteen more miles.

I check behind me, to see how my red shadow of a VW reacts to my assholery. What I see, the crimson hood of his car nearly disappeared, he's so close to me.

For a second, I swear I see a nose hair coming from the old man, somewhat balding. His eyes squint the way James Bond villains do when they hatch up a master plan.

This man, I watch as he bites his lower lip hard, teeth glaring, and his body shifts back into the seat. My own car jerks forward.

"What the hell is your problem, jackwipe?" I shout into the desert air.

The man responds with a honk and another tap.

"Fuck you, too, you old coot." I press harder on the accelerator with the intent to move off to the next lane, the slower lane, but the car does not accelerate.

Turning, looking over my shoulder, there's this guy, his pointed nose peering as close to his windshield as his seatbelt will let him, and he accelerates faster. He matches me, mile per hour for mile per hour.

"Are you trying to kill us?" I scream.

My foot presses to the floor, knees ache from the sudden movement. The stagnation of three hours of holding my entire right leg in the exact position left my ass numb. Even the sudden onslaught of adrenaline from the attack cannot resurrect my ass muscles.

His car offers a love tap to mine, throwing my head and shoulders forward, then backward. I feel confused, like my brain was bouncing from one side of my head to the other.

"What is wrong with you?"

This man, his face disappears in the chaos of moving car and shadows draped across his face. All I see—no shit like some kind of cartoon or something—is a white smile, pearly white and gleaming a bright white flash of a star.

And I swear, for a second, I see a flash of nose, teeth, of dark black hair—her hair—and then it's back to the old man.

No other recourse than to drive like I stole this car. I shove the pedal to the floor so hard I may actually break it.

This crazy old coot, he keeps right with me, nearing my bumper. My heart beats faster, pulsing with the speed of a hummingbird as he inches nearer and nearer.

Time to gun it, go for gold.

My foot lays off the pedal, in a split second, finding the brake and turning the car into a spin.

A bright red lightning bolt blazes past my car. The squeal of his brakes echoes into the distance, returning back to my own ears.

I don't bother looking back. I see no point to it. I'm sure he's chasing me.

Only one thing to do: hightail it out of there until I get to a safe place, maybe somewhere with police or law enforcement of any kind.

A sheriff's department or department of corrections will work, too.

To calm my nerves, I flick on the radio and let the buzzing static air turn into a whiny country twang. Not my type of music, but it means I'm closer to society, closer to freedom.

The simple tune hangs in my memory like I wrote it, so I hum along and pray in the back of my mind. Sure God probably won't hear it, but if he does, at least he'll know I was thinking about him when I get into an accident.

Miles of green pave the distance just beside the road.

Miles and miles of green that I've already passed before. I have no choice but to follow it again, pass it all again. Maybe take a bit of time to appreciate the environment.

And though I didn't mean to, my eyes slip into the rearview mirror. The view is nothing but green and blue. Dark trees stand watch over the roads, sentinels guarding the roads against too much sunshine.

My brain feels tired, dizzy, like it's rotating on the tip of my spine. Closing my eyes, I count to ten, slow.

In the mirror, nothing. No demon car. No evil bald men. Nothing trying to kill me.

"There is no evil in the mirror."

This I learned in cognitive behavioral therapy.

"There is no evil in the mirror. No evil in the mirror."

I grudgingly move my eyes to stare directly at myself in the mirror. Slow gaze, concentrating on the green color of my eyes, the brown outlines. The way the lines fan out, rotating around my iris. "Nothing wants to kill me."

And for the next few minutes, my heart slows down to a thump-thump, to a regular sixty beats per minute heart rate.

The sun has traveled from just above me to sitting behind me now, the bottom rays coming into my car, meeting my eyes off the rearview mirror. If I want to make it to Saraday soon, I'll have to make up some time.

Just to make sure, because I really can't handle a heart attack right now, I take one more quick glance at the mirror. Or at least try to.

My eyes look at the black plastic rim of the mirror, the safety of the frame telling me it's okay to stop.

Take a breather.

I hold my breath, deep in my lungs and letting it expand into my chest, like a balloon ready to pop. Exhale, a long steady stream.

Peer up. Up. Up some more.

The top of my hair, my shiny forehead—from sweat or grease, I can't tell—to my eyebrows and eyes.

Dark green.

No horrors in the mirror. No one wants to kill me.

"No evil in the mirror. Remember what the doctor taught you." Take another breath, look behind me, over my shoulder.

No one. Green and dirt and black roads behind me. Nothing.

With a breath that feels like a soothing mint breeze down my throat, I turn the wheel of the car, pull the shift into drive, and turn around to Saraday.

4

JAMES

Saraday, South Carolina has a history that runs deeper than the Confederate South. Today it's almost two hundred square miles, divided nearly in half by the end of an interstate to the Atlantic Ocean.

The lumbering green trees, reminiscent of a modern Jurassic Park, pull most of the city folk to retire in these parts. The housing prices will typically seal the deal once the old ones decide this is where they want to die.

As I enter the town's limits, the sign has the same bullshit lie it had when I left nearly thirteen years ago: Population 1953. That number? It might as well be written on a white dry erase board. No one stays here. Not since the major industries—wood and fishing— were sold and sold again and again.

That's the reason my own family left. No money, no interest in staying.

Just from the Welcome to Saraday sign to the first grocery mart, I counted three cashing places and a pawn mart. Suspiciously close to each other.

While the locals know this place as home, the other neighboring towns look at this humble little village as a creepy, creepy hamlet.

When I went to school, our field trips took us out to the middle of the fields. Literal fields. There, we got a chance to take our lunches, look at the trees, watch the snakes slither from branch to branch.

Yes, snakes. Branches. You heard me. Nearly every northern family doesn't last long out in these parts.

Sometimes during a threat of hurricanes or tornadoes, my dad took me out into the storms and bought about three hundred dollars of two-by-fours and nails. The next year—or just a few months down the road some years—my dad forgot about the extra boards and told me to buy more.

Got wood? We did.

You may have also noticed our adorable town on TV shows the likes of Rescue 911, Hidden Mysteries of the South, and Unsolved Mysteries. We hold the distinct honor of housing three of the top ten most wanted rapists and sexual predators in the nation from 1996 to 1998. In 1999, we had two of them put to death according to South Carolina law. Lethal injection. Texas, eat your heart out.

Raising Canes retirement community. Correction, Raising Canes Assisted Living Community. My grandfather lives here, Pop Pop Thurston. My mother's father.

Today, seniors play tennis to lead more active, fulfilling lives. At least this is what my mother says. It made her feel better when we finally committed my Pop Pop to the home.

For what it's worth, it's easier to send someone into assisted living care when you live nearly a thousand miles away.

When I arrive at Raising Canes through the first set of glass doors into the foyer, a man in blue jeans, white shirt and almost no attention to his hair stamps his hand onto the counter. "What the hell do you mean he's not here? I just saw him yesterday! Ewing White! I know he's here!"

The black woman at the counter shakes her head, pretends to type something on the keyboard, then looks at him. "I'm sorry," she says. "Nothing here." Her deep black eyes feign a smile, her unpainted lips pull back into a smirk.

The man storms off, his shoulder bumping into mine. A trail of morning-old B.O. and expensive fashion-magazine cologne follows along. "Excuse me, jackass," he says.

"That's that good old Southern hospitality I'm used to." With a smile, leaning over the counter, I ask, "Is um, Raymond Thurston still here?" I pause. Look up toward my forehead, pretend that I'm thinking. "Room sixteen, I think?"

Smile. Pretend to be nice but forgettable. Just interesting to get into the front fucking door and see this old man.

The woman stares into the computer monitor, a pale white glow changes her thick, caked-on makeup into an almost purplish version of a real human being.

Her fingers click click on the keyboard too fast to see what she's really typing.

"So, there really is a typing class for secretaries?" I ask.

"Excuse me?"

"Find anything?" I'll admit, my shoulders pull forward, hide my chest and for a minute, I'm afraid she'll reach over the desk and end my life.

"Oh," she says with a smile. "Typing class." Her fingers wiggle in the air, typing on a fake keyboard. "You're funny, Mr., um...."

"Green," I say. "James Green."

"I'm Suzy," she says and extends a wide open hand to shake mine.

"Nice to meet you," she says. "Raymond doesn't get many guests. Not that he's lonely or anything." Her smile tries to comfort me.

I don't fight the feeling.

"Good to know," I say. "Where is he?"

"I'll show you," she says. As she stands, it becomes clear that this woman loves to eat, crumbs falling off the rounded curves of her breasts and could-be-pregnant belly. She grabs a clipboard from the counter and hands it to me. "Just sign in here, please," she says, taps on the paper too fast for me to see.

We go through a series of doorways down a long hall with painted walls, murals.

"We've had to step up some of the security a few years ago," she says. "So I hope you don't mind me taking you to see him." Her eyes measure me from the soles of my feet to my forest green eyes. She winks.

"No, I don't mind at all." Keep your eyes on the hallway in front of you. Stay on the non-reflective surfaces of the walls. "Nice mural," I say. All small talk, which is why I don't pay attention when Suzy turns on her inner tour guide and feeds me information I really don't give a shit about.

"What happened a few years ago?" I ask.

"We had a patient kill himself during a fire alarm." The nurse waddles slower until coming to a complete standstill. "We're not supposed to talk about it," she says, "but someone about your age came in, upset everyone, killed his mother and then left with the dead body."

"Jesus Christ," I say.

"Oh trust me," she says. "Jesus wants nothing to do with that one. That was the work of the Devil." Her eyes peer into mine, deep down, the wet, reflective surfaces of her eyes shine some light back into my face.

I turn away. "So, um," I point at the door. "This it?"

5

JAMES

Pop Pop sits in front of his television, flicking through channels so fast I doubt he's actually listening to a damn thing.

With him sitting on his bed, he looks so large, huge even, compared to the rest of the room. It can't be bigger than my room when I was a little boy. Maybe nine by nine. Probably.

The room looks to be pre-decorated because I don't notice a single thing in here that belonged to my Pop Pop. The dark blue horizontal blinds work well to keep the light out of here, but the rest of the room has been painted a dentist office white. Bright, pearly. Everything you'd need to blind yourself on a sunny day.

I tap on the door, saying "Don't bother, there's nothing on at this time of day."

Pop Pop smiles at me. His wrinkled finger presses the power button and he tosses the controller onto his bed. "Shit," he says. "Don't I know it." His arms open wide. "How is your sister?"

He smells like mint, breath mint of some kind and I'm instantly taken back to my days at the old house, that same house I helped clean out a few days ago.

"She's been dead a few years now."

Mom warned me that the man I was going to see was not the Pop Pop I had once remembered.

A sudden sadness crashes over Pop Pop's face. His lower lip quivers, barely able to keep still. "When did that happen?"

"It was three years ago," I say.

"How? Why?" he says.

Never in my life had I imagined he would react this strongly to her death. Again. And again. And again.

"Listen Pop Pop, we need to talk, okay?"

Pop Pop regains some of his composure, his eyes remain glassy, however. Looking deep within them, bits of fleshy pink inner eyelid comes apparent. The poor man is so wrinkled he's starting to fold inside out.

"But I've been okay," I say. His bed feels firm and nothing like his old bed underneath my ass muscles. "How are you holding up?"

Pop Pop smiles, looks down at his feet and then looks up at me. It was his trademark, this look. Like something out of a fifties movie, maybe even a James Dean moment. It was a surefire way to know he was lying to me. "Enough about me," he says. He turns to look at me, keeping my eyes on my every motion.

"Do you?" I point to the shades in the window. "Do you mind?"

"You're still doing this shit?" he says. You could hear him rolling his eyes.

"No, not really." I turn to face him, "Alright, yes. Yes, I am." My instinct is to sit next to him, try to be closer to him and get the information I came here for, but he won't let me. "It's sort of what I need to talk to you about."

"About your pissy little girly shit?" he says.

"It's pronounced pho-bee-ya, Pop Pop."

"Is that what you call being a little bitch about a little mirror game." He shakes his head. "Just a little scared puppy."

"Pop Pop!"

"You're a bitch. You're a wimp. Afraid of your imaginary friend."

"Imaginary, ay?" I hold up a finger, signaling hold on and reach into my jacket pocket. "What about her?"

6

POP POP

I don't know what my grandson was trying to pull with that stunt, pulling this picture out in front of me like I'm going to just jump up and scream my heart out.

"This is what I'm afraid of," he says. James musta been nervous. His hands shook like Janice's. She's this girl down the hallway, has Parkinson's or something or another.

"Hold that straight," I says. "I can barely see it." My arthritic hands grab for the picture, but he won't let me take it. "Will you give it here!" I demand. "Give me that, James."

Finally, he lets go. What I see is a face I hadn't seen in, Jesus H. Christ, fifty years, maybe?

"Where did you get this?" I says.

James's hands shake so much, he has to shove them into his pockets to keep them still. His arms and elbows are thrust deep into his sides. You know, to keep from making it look like he's nervous. "It was when we were going to through your stuff. Mom said we needed to clean some stuff out."

He tries to keep it all a secret from me, but they don't have to. I know what's going on. I'm not going back to the house.

I never was going back, at least that wasn't their intention.

The thing about having a bad hip is, you have a tendency to fall down. And that I did. A lot. Lots more times and eventually everyone starts worrying about me. They says I needed someone to look after me, that they were too busy.

They says that I need something to keep me busy and safe so I don't fall down anymore.

Raising Canes is their answer. It's their answer to everything. Any time I crack wise at the dinner table, they says I'm going to Raising Canes. When I said I was missing my wife, Suzette, they says I'm going to Raising Canes.

One time. One time I shit myself I was laughing so hard and didn't want to go downstairs to the bathroom.

Whoops, they says. Must be something wrong with you. Off to Raising Canes.

The whole lot of them wanted me gone. For what, I don't know.

Maybe it's because they were digging for gold, maybe for some secret buried treasure they thought I had? It was probably Suzette who gave them that idea. She always thought I was hiding something.

"Why are you digging through my things?" I says.

James uses his dainty little fingers to politely place the photo on my lap. From here, I can finally see my picture. Never needed glasses, not me. My whole family, we had strong eyes. Strong seers, every one of us.

"Mom said—"

"I don't care what your mother says," I tells him. "You don't have to go digging through my things. It's rude."

James sighs and gives up. He always gave up too soon. Never fought for nothing, that kid.

"Listen, Pop Pop. I know you thought I was joking and messing around with you." The skin on his face turns sweaty and red. He runs both his hands through his thick brown hair—a Thurston family trademark—and lets a long stream of air come out of his lips. "But this girl," he says, pointing at my lap. "That's who I see all the time."

"You're full of bullshit," I says. "You don't know what you're talking about."

"Who is she?" he asks. I already know from the pansy tears dropping down his cheeks that he's not going to let this rest.

"She was a girl, James. That's all."

"If she was just a girl, then why are you holding her in that picture?"

"I'm holding her because she was cold."

"Bullshit. If you don't tell me soon, I think more people are going to die."

"Don't make me ask the nurse for some soap for your mouth." Leave it to my own grandson to think he's being cute.

"For Christ's sake, Pop Pop, Grandma wouldn't tell me who she was. Why won't you?"

"Because it's not important," I tells him. I flip the picture over, but not before looking at it. Her hair, that flaming auburn hair that hung over her shoulders and cheeks like she was hiding something.

I'll tell you what she was hiding, she was hiding some dark secrets. That girl, she was crazy and I was crazy over her.

"I'm not leaving until I get the truth," he says. As he says this, he plops his butt flat on the chair. "So?"

"So? So what? One click of a button and I could have your girly ass thrown out of here."

"You could, but would you want Mom to find out?"

My face stays serious. It says "Yes, I double dog dare you" just to throw him off, but my heart says no. He can't know that I'm trying to scare him. Maybe get some real heart in that girly bitch of a grandson.

"Do you really want to know?" I asks him.

James nods, grabs hold of his chair and he smiles. Immediately as I'm about to start telling him this story, he stands up and takes the pillow cover off my pillow—my biggest one at that—and covers the mirror on my wall.

"Just in case," he says.

"In case of what? You need to check your hair?"

"Pop Pop, my phobia." His head cocks forward. His eyebrows raise up, like that's really going to help me take him more serious.

"If you have to know, James, you might say she was someone I cared about. You might say we were close." I swallow my heart and my fear with a big, dry gulp. "You might also say she was the worst thing to happen to this family."

7

POP POP

You've heard that story, "The Ugly Duckling," right? Pretty sure your mom read it to you when you was little. Well, if you remember that story any, then you might understand why Madeline was such a shock to us boys in ninth grade.

I know you don't want to hear this much, but back then, we was about fourteen years old, hormones—except we didn't call them hormones back then—hormones was surging through us and we just couldn't wait to go steady with our first girl.

Well, some of us couldn't wait to go steady. Some of the boys like Mo Landau, he had already dated his first girl. Kissed her in eighth grade like he was hot shit. Walked around like it too.

After that, all the girls wanted to flock to Mo. They heard from his first girl that he was great kisser. Funny now that I think about it. He turned out to be, you know. A little funny.

Anyway, back in those days, I remember coming back from Spring Break thinking this was going to be my year. I was fourteen and was just starting to grow a mustache. Sure they was little hairs, almost transparent on my upper lip, but I worked hard to get those hairs. Hell, I practically combed them in the mirror before I went to school.

In those hallways, we had our lockers. Mine was the first one next to my history class, so I was always taking my time in the halls, watching the girls walk by and trying to talk to them.

I'd sit there and practice what I'd say. You know, if you wanted to get the girls to notice you, you had to stand out, show some real balls.

With my new mustache, I thought I'd stand out for sure.

Anyway, we all get back from Spring Break, and I swear to you, half that town came back with a tan. You'd think it was Hollywood, California, or something. Everyone—and I mean everyone—went to Florida or Alabama or North Carolina for vacation. The families with the most money, they went to New York to their other homes.

Me? Your great grandpop didn't have much money back then working in the mines and all, so we stayed in. I worked on my basketball practice and your great grandmother baked till the cows came home.

Those days, I barely saw my dad. He worked in the neighboring towns, sometimes going on fishing boats off the coast of Charleston during the summer and working the mines in the summer. So, I was left to myself.

I tell you this because it was me trying to stuff my basketball back into my locker when the damned thing rolled out and bounced down that hallway. It must have been karma or fate, but that ball bounced all the way down the hallway.

I knocked juniors and seniors out of the way, shoving them to one side and apologizing after I had already been a safe distance out of arm's length down the hall. "Whoops, sorry." "Chasing after my ball, sorry!"

When I finally reach that ball, I realize there are toes—toes from open-toed sandals—right behind and underneath my ball. My fingers gripped the sides of the ball, surprisingly sweaty—my fingers, not the ball—and there she was in all of her swan-like glory: Madeline.

When she was only about seven-years-old, Madeline was the type of girl who liked to come to school wearing pink dresses with some kind of animal on them. Sometimes it was a horse, sometimes it was a puppy. Sometimes a kitty.

Honestly, it didn't matter what kind of animal it was, we gave her shit for it.

For all we knew, it was her favorite animal, or maybe her mother made her those clothes. Nobody asked because nobody cared. We were kids, and making fun of each other was what kids did back in those days.

So she came to school in those dresses and her hair all done up in dirty pigtails. I mean dirty, James. The kind of dirt that you see in vacuum cleaner bags. I think once a teacher actually called the police on her parents. They said she was maybe neglected, left at home and told to eat cat food out of a can. No fork. No spoon or nothing.

That's what they say, anyway. To this day, I don't know if I believed any of it, even after meeting her.

I gripped the ball on the sides, pulled it up and held it close to my little pigeon chest. "Sorry about that," I said.

"Hi, Ray," she says to me.

"You know who I am?" Her green, green eyes stole my attention, like staring at the moss on the Everglades. A murky green that looked brownish depending on how you looked at them. Her smile, her little lips pointed at the edges of her mouth. It was love at first sight.

"Of course, I do, Ray. It's me, Madeline."

And I shit you not, I could have dropped my ball right there and not even known it. I stumble backward, waiting for my heart to start up again.

"Madeline? Madeline as in Madeline Schemel? " I says. "Wow, you're, um, you're looking good."

Maddy smiled, looked into my eyes and nodded. She didn't need to say anything. Her eyes said it all.

Heh, now that I think about it, her entire body said everything I needed to know.

Her hair hung behind her head in one of those tight ponytails, clean and brown. Her skirt was a soft baby pink, but her shirt was white and beautiful. Really bringing out her best features, you know what I mean?

Boy, those were some good features. Your grandmother never had features like that, God rest her soul.

"Did you just transfer back here?" I asks her. "I don't remember seeing you around."

Madeline smiled and blushed a color of pink you only see on roses. "No, silly. I've been going to Saraday High all year long."

You know, I thought she was mad at me at first for asking her that question. Later that summer, she told me she was really flirting with me. She just didn't know how, not being pretty and all.

"Oh wow," I says. "So uh, where are you going?"

The hallways begin to clear out about now, probably because the bell was fixing to ring above us. I didn't know. All I know is she's standing in front of me, and I felt like I was the center of her world.

It was the first time I was the center of anything except Monkey in the Middle.

"I'm going to history," she says.

"Did you just transfer there?" I asks her.

Sure as shit, she says to me, "No."

Talk about embarrassing. As penance, she let me walk her to our next class and she took her seat, three seats in front of mine in the center row.

From behind, I stared at the back of her head for the next fifty minutes, not taking notes. Not paying attention, no nothing.

All my mind will let me think about in my little fourteen-year-old head is how much she had changed, and how nobody else seemed to notice so I had to act fast if I wanted to see what other features she might have grown into.

8

POP POP

When I sit down at the lunch table, the boys all start squawking about the new girl in the school.

"Yeah, yeah, I met the new girl," I says. I take special note to glance them all in the eyes, let them know I'm serious. "She's kinda cute," I says.

"Kinda cute?" Billy says. His hands slam the table in tight fists. "She's not a bad looking broad," he says. "She new here?"

I struggle with how I'm going to answer this. I think that I could go ahead and tell everyone who she is and catch hell for liking Madeline, or I could go ahead and lie and keep it a secret. You know, in case I end up with her sometime.

"Yeah, yeah. She's new here," I says. "Transferred from out of town somewheres."

"Man, they know how to grow them out there, don't they, Billy?" Tommy says. Tommy's freckled face peers at all of us, looking for his approval from Billy or from me. Poor guy was the littlest out of all of us. All he wanted was maybe some attention, some recognition that he, too, could be one of the big boys.

"Yeah, Tommy. They know how to grow them," I says, patting him on the forearms.

Tommy sits back, content and beaming from ear to ear.

"So you looking at asking her out?" Billy asks. His eyes move steady in my direction, trying to nail my own eyes down with a deadlock stare. "What you thinking?"

"I'm thinking yeah, I think I might just go talk to her. Maybe ask her out."

"Where are you going to ask her out to? Movies?" Tommy smiles, like he just caught me in a lie or something.

"You're a freaking moron, Tommy," I says. "I can just take her to a party or something. There's always a party, right?"

"I don't know of no parties right now. Not this weekend," says Billy. Now his smile, he knows he's gonna make this kinda difficult for me.

"Well, you gotta do something, Ray. You gotta ask her out. She's so," he pauses for the right word. Then, with a smile, he says, "Different."

"Calm down there, Tommy," I says. "Or maybe I might think you want to ask her out."

Tommy sits back in his plastic seat and looks around, pulling at his shirt collar and stretching it out to about three times its original size. "I don't know what you're talking about," he says. "Hey, are they selling pudding today?" He gets up to check.

"That Tommy," I says. "Some days I'm surprised he even finds the front door in the morning."

I waited around her last class for about a whole fifteen minutes trying to figure out just how I was going to ask this girl to go steady with me. I mean, it was a big thing for a fourteen-year-old.

So I waited around for the bell to ring for the last period. It wasn't easy, by the way, staying out of everyone's view.

We didn't have hall monitors in those days, just responsible kids because we were smarter than you morons these days. We knew how to sneak around and we knew how to get in trouble without killing anyone or hurting anyone.

It was all just fun and games. We didn't mean no harm in it or anything.

When finally the bell rang, I had to slow down my breathing, you know, to keep from having a heart attack right then and there.

I mean, I wasn't that nervous or nothing, but it was a big deal. If Madeline said no, then I'd be known around the school as a big old loser. And I couldn't have her maybe going out with Billy or nothing. That would be too embarrassing. Imagining her with her hands wrapped around his, walking down the hallways all cute and cuddly like.

And the meanwhile, I'm on the sides of the hallway, watching these two make out and Tommy's clowning me about how I should have been dating her and how I'm a bigger loser than he is.

Not that he'd say that. Big doofus was too much of a doofus to know he's a doofus.

I waited, kept my eyes peeled for Madeline, looking at her through the crowd of kids leaving their Spanish class. It was a popular class, that Spanish class was. At least it seemed to be, with all of these kids pouring out into the hallway like they just left a clown car.

Then finally, I heard around me, "Ray, what are you doing here?" It was Madeline, her beautiful green eyes just pulling me into her world.

"Uh, heya there, Maddy," I says. "I was just looking for you."

"Looking for me?" she says. Then she did this cute little thing, clutching her books closer to her features, covering them up and looking down all bashful and shy. "What for?"

And don't let those smiles confuse you none, when a girl asks you that type of question, they already know the answer. They are just waiting for you to say something.

"I was wondering," I says. And man, those features were just so amazing in that blouse. "I was wondering, well, if you'd like to go out sometime. You know, maybe go grab a burger or something."

Madeline, she takes a second to look at me, and like in slow motion, her red pouty lips, trying to be cutesy with me, they turn upwards into this big crescent smile big as the moon and she says, "Yes, Ray. I'd love to."

It took me everything I had to keep from wanting to grab her right then and there and kiss her. Back then, it was bad form. You had to at least woo a girl first. You couldn't just grab her, do what you want.

Bad form and just plain rude.

I remember stuttering after that, talking to everybody and just could not wait to tell Billy and Tommy what was going on.

"That's wonderful," I says. "Can we go out tonight? Maybe around six?"

"My family is having dinner at that time, Ray. You can come over if you want."

And dammit, I could have had a second heart attack at that moment. I swear to this day my left arm started feeling numb and tingly. "I don't know if that's such a great idea right now, Madeline. I mean, we ain't even gone out yet," I says.

She blushes, studies my face with her green, green eyes. Each time she blinks, I feel like her gaze digs deeper and deeper into my brain. "Then at least come and pick me up?" she says. With a smile like that, her big pouty lips, it was impossible to say no.

"Uh, yeah," I says. "I can definitely do that."

It was one of the happiest days of my life, I tells you. It probably shouldn't have been, but I was the happiest boy in Saraday. I had been the first boy to ask out the amazingly beautiful new girl.

And don't go telling me that I already said she wasn't new. I knew that, and she knew that. But as far as anyone else knew in that school, Madeline Schemel was brand spanking new and mine for the taking.

So after asking her out, I give her a pat on the shoulder, because I was a lame moron and I had no idea what to do.

Come on, I was fourteen for Christ's sake. What did I know about girls and about relationships?

But I did know about how to be a young boy in love.

Yes, I said love. You understand, I was fourteen. If anything made me romanticize about having my dick sucked, then it made me fall in love.

Don't lie and say you never felt that way.

"This girl must have meant a lot to you," James says.

"I never said that," I says to him. "And don't you go repeatin it, either. I just look back at those years like some of the best of my life. It's been a long time since I dug that far back of my memories," I says. "Now where was I?"

So I ran home and couldn't wait to tell my momma. Your great grandma was a sight to behold. A beautiful woman who held herself higher than her neighbors and looked after her family like a real woman should.

It was when I came home that one afternoon, damn near out of breath, that I came home to amazing cookies and cakes.

"Ray," she says to me. "Come sit down." As I sit down, she hands me a plate and a glass of milk. "Why don't you get yourself some cookies and come sit."

My mom wasn't the talkative type, so I knew this was something out of the ordinary. We Thurstons are the type to write letters when we break up. Shoot first and never ask questions, if you know what I'm saying.

All my life I heard my mom say "I love you," but it was always in passing.

I see that look in your eyes, boy. I know what yer thinking, and it's not the same, okay?

So my mother, she sits down next to me and looks right into my eyes and says that she needed to tell me something important.

"We're going to have to move away out of Saraday," she says to me. Her eyes are trying as hard as they can to look sad and lonely. Maybe try to feel my pain and reflect my emotions back at me.

This was how she dealt with things, you see. She never wanted to really show she was sad or happy, so she mirrored everything back to you. She had no emotions herself, only your emotions.

If you were happy, she was happy. If you were sad, she was sad. Got annoying as hell with a lot of people in the household every Thanksgiving.

"Why?" I asked. "Why we gotta move?"

"Your father needs another job. The mines aren't going to last long. And they're dangerous." My mother rests her silky hands on mine. "Now eat your cookies, dear."

I let my hands slip out of her grip and clutch a golden chocolate chip cookie. The whole thing was so moist and big—just the way she knew I liked them—that no crumbs fell off it as I lifted it to your mouth.

I wish your Maw Maw learned how to make cookies like my mother. Let me tell you, the crap you're eating now is shit compared to your grandmaw's cookies.

My mother went back to fixing the dishes or cleaning something around the house or something or another. And I just sat there, sat there completely confused and dumbfounded. Then I started to think something that made me feel even worse.

Looking back now, I realize I was only fourteen, and it was okay for me to think this way. But looking back, I saw that I was mostly sad about losing my first real girlfriend. I was just about to get to first base—though I wasn't sure what first base was back at that age—but I was determined to get there soon.

"Mom!" I calls out to her. "Mom! When are we moving?"

"Soon, dear," is all I could get out of your grandmaw. Her curls bounce as she says this to me in her spunky and happy for no apparent reason.

Like I said, your grandmaw didn't handle emotions too well.

I didn't stick around for dinner. I left the house as soon as I realized that my mother wasn't keeping her typical overbearing eagle eye on me. I couldn't stand the blank, emotionless mirror in my mom's face, and I didn't want to risk yelling at my dad.

I knew it wasn't his fault, but I wanted to blame someone anyway. I guess I needed to blame someone for this.

I ran. Straight to my friends' house. I was lucky, they were only a few blocks away from me and I welcomed the chance to exercise and get these nerves straightened out with a good run. Keep myself out of breath and too tired to be pissed off about everything.

When I reached Billy's house, I tried to regain my composure as quick as I could. Patted down my hair and wiped my face with my sleeves a few times, you know, in case I was crying. Then, with a quivering little hand, I knocked on the door and waited for someone to come by.

But no one did. Not a single goddamn person.

"Billy!" I shouts out to the windows. "Billy! You here?"

But nothing. No answers from nobody.

Then I decides to do what any self-respecting young boy would do and climb that house.

I remembered Billy's dad keeps a ladder nearby to trim the hedges and trees in case they grew too high. So I drag it to Billy's upstairs window and climb on up.

"Billy!" I cry out, rapping on the window with my knuckles. Hard at first, then harder still. "Billy!"

"I think they went to dinner," says a voice from down below me. It was little Tommy, hands on his hips and squinting at me all the way from the ground floor. "Whatcha doing up there?"

"I was hoping Billy was home," I says. I climbed back down, thinking this could be the last time that I climb down those steps.

This could be the last time that I was stepping on Billy's lawn.

The last time I could be seeing Tommy's silly freckled face.

"Yeah, I don't think Billy's there," he says. Tommy digs through his pockets and brings out a couple of quarters. "You wanna go get some ice cream from the corner store?"

I'll admit, I have nothing to do at that point, nowhere to go until at least six, so I just nod my head yes and follow Tommy down the road.

"You look a little upset, Ray," he says. "What's the matter?"

"I don't wanna talk about it," I says. I snatch a quarter from his hands as he's flipping it in his fingers like some mobster from the movies.

"Are you sure?" he says. "Maybe I can help."

"Trust me, Tommy, I don't think you can help much with this one."

And the rest of the talk, we are quiet. Calm, even. No words are exchanged and it's funny, but for the first time, I felt like I had a real chance to clear my head.

No worries about my girlfriend—whether I had one or not—and no worries about losing my friends.

"What kind of ice cream you want?" says Tommy. He fumbles through his pockets again, pulling out more quarters.

"Just how many of those things you got in there? You go steal from a bank or something?"

Tommy laughs and pokes around through the layer of silver on his palm. "One. Two." He looks up to me, smiles. "I have about four," he says. "That should be enough to get us an ice cream, don't ya think?"

"That should be enough to get us an ice cream and maybe a soda if we wanted to split one," I says. I didn't see no harm in trying to get more than just ice cream. I was moving away, dammit, I deserved something.

So we goes into the store and Tommy grabs an ice cream. "Take one," he says, opening the door to the fridge for me.

I pick a cone, covered with chocolate because that's the only thing I know that will keep me calm right now. It's been forever since I had a cone in those days.

We weren't poor, really, but your great grandpop didn't have much money on account of the mines losing their business.

"Thank you, Tommy," I says to him. "I didn't expect you to show up and help cheer me up."

Tommy takes one big goofy lick of his ice cream. "You don't have to thank me," he says. "It's what friends are for, right?" He takes another big goofy lick like a Labrador Retriever licking a ham bone. I even think a Labrador's tongue is smaller than Tommy's.

"I think I'm moving soon, Tommy," I says. The speed that it all came out, so suddenly, surprised even me.

I swear I must have put my hands over my mouth to keep from spilling out anything more.

"Moving where, Ray?" he says. And as I watch him lap at his ice cream, I notice that Tommy's not as shaken up about this whole thing as much as I thought he would be. Tommy's always been a sweet kid, so I guess I expected more heart, more emotions.

"I don't know," I says. "My mom didn't say much, just that we'd be moving soon."

"When you moving, Ray?"

Again, I just shrug. "She didn't say," I says.

Then, Tommy laughs. Inside his dark mouth, I can see parts of his ice cream that he hasn't swallowed yet still on his tongue and in his cheeks. "You even sure you're moving?" he says with a laugh.

I don't know what comes over me, but I grab Tommy's shirt in my hands, my fingers digging deep into his shirt, and I push him to the ground. "Shut up, Tommy. Yes, I'm moving. Alright? I swear I'm moving."

My friend lay on the grassy ground, his hands holding him up and his half-eaten ice cream cone melting in a pile of rocks next to him. "You made me drop my ice cream, Ray."

I swear Tommy looked sadder over losing that ice cream than losing me.

"Well, you shouldn't have been smart about it, okay? I told you I was moving, and I'm moving."

Tommy wipes his swollen red eyes with the back of his dirty hands. "I'm sorry, Ray. You didn't have to push me, though."

"I know I didn't, Tommy." I take a big swallow of my pride. "I'm sorry."

"It's okay." Tommy's big old goofy smile comes back. He still forgot to swallow his ice cream all the way.

"You got chocolate on your teeth," I says.

"I do?" he says. Tommy smiles a big grin and wipes his teeth with the bottom of his shirt, exposing his skinny belly and shiny buttons on his pants.

"Those new pants, Tommy?" I says.

"Sure are," he says. "Mom just bought them new yesterday."

"When did your family get so much money?" I says. I watch Tommy count out another two quarters in his hands and he looks at me.

"I don't know, I guess we always had the money."

"Why don't you act like you got more money. You know, snobby and dressed in suits and all that?"

"And make myself look like a penguin?" says Tommy. "That's just stupid." Tommy takes his hand over his heart and stands over the ice cream.

"Whatcha doing?" I ask.

Tommy raises his finger to his mouth to tell me to shush and he bows his head. I can't hear what he's whispering to himself or to the ice cream, but it sounds like he's telling a story or something. "Amen," he says and makes a cross, shoulder to shoulder, forehead to his balls. "You want anything else?" he says.

At six, I tells Tommy that I got my date, and he whispers over to me that he's wishing me luck, and that I should feel lucky since Billy wants to date her too.

"Over my dead body," I says. "Nobody wanted her when she was Madeline Schemel, the ugly girl."

Madeline's house had to be one of the biggest on the block, easy. Such a big house, it was intimidating to stand in front of it. Even more intimidating to knock on it.

Swear, I hold my breath for about two minutes before I finally take the chance and knock on the door.

When nobody comes to the door, I hold my ear against the door, listening for signs of life. "Come on, Madeline," I says. "Don't stand me up."

When the door opens, I'm still standing there like an idiot with my head where the door should be. "Can I help you?" a woman says.

"Uh, yeah." I don't know what to do, so I take my hands and hold them, rubbing them against each other like the Nervous Nelly I am. "Um, is Madeline here?" I says.

The woman at the door—must be her mom or someone like that—looks at me like she'd rather slap me and send me away than let me inside their pristine home. "Yes," she says. She stands by the door and motions for me to come in. "Yes, she is."

And this house, it looks real old, like Civil War old. It was a gorgeous house, looks really rich. Nothing makes a boy feel low than finding out everybody in the world seems to have money except for you.

Worse yet, you even gotta move because your dad can't earn enough money.

"Madeline!" the woman screams. Her massive house echoes her voice all the way up to the hallway and back into my ears.

From upstairs, I hear a woman scream something back, but I'm too far away to understand what these two are yelling at each other.

"She'll be right here," the woman says. "Can I get you anything to drink?" she says.

"Just a beer, please," I says and the look on this woman's face, I thought she was gonna kill me. "I'm sorry," I says. "It was a joke. A bad one. I'm sorry."

I apologize like six more times as the woman walks away from me.

Since nobody invited me to sit down on their ash gray leather furniture, I just stand up and run my hands over the leather. It's as real as any leather jacket, but thinner. My little fingers could probably poke a hole through it if I felt pissed off enough.

"Be careful with that," says a voice, and I look up. It's Madeline, looking stunning and beautiful as ever.

My jaw opens, and I'm sure I'm going to say something, but I forget what as I watch her come down the steps one by one. As she lowers to the next step, her features bounce tight against her chest.

And all I'm thinking is, I really am glad they aren't here, but I wish Tommy and Billy could see this girl.

"I'm. Sorry?" I says. My tongue feels too big to be in my mouth, and my lips don't wanna work for nothing.

"It's okay," she says. "I've dug little holes all over that couch." Madeline falls to the bottom step and leans over to kiss me on the cheek. "That's how I know it's so fragile." She smiles.

At the same time, my heart feels like a little squirrel running around in my chest. While I want to calm it down, I love how this feels.

"So, where are we going?" she says.

"I don't know," I tells her. "I was thinking maybe the park."

She frowns.

"—Or maybe the park?"

Madeline's lips smile and melt right through my tough guy persona.

I'm not sure how much experience you have with girls, see, but they aren't as clear on their intentions as guys. You see, it's killer for guys to ask "Am I supposed to hold her hand?" or "Am I supposed to hold her." These are things that young women just won't tell you. Then they get mad at you when you don't do what they want.

These are the things I'm telling you, James. Take notes for crying out loud.

But as we walk there that night, I realize that I really did seem to like her. A lot. As we walk to the park, she wraps her arms around her like she's cold, which is preposterous. It's a beautiful South Carolina night. A beautiful and not too muggy seventy degrees out that evening. Warm enough for a light coat, maybe.

But Madeline had put on a long sleeve blouse, so I was pretty sure she could not be that cold. Besides, even I didn't have a coat.

So, I do the next best thing.

"Mind if I warm you up a little bit?" I says and reach overall smooth like and put my hands on her shoulders.

She tenses up at first, but then relaxes as she feels my body heat against hers. We're walking, step for step, next to each other like we choreographed it the night before. "Feel better?" I says.

She blushes, a beautiful red on her cheeks, like someone had dusted rose petals over her cheeks. It could not have been a more beautiful night, I tell you.

So we go to the park and climb under the metal posts that tell us we aren't supposed to be there after hours. Governments those days didn't trust any of us kids. Said we were up to no good like necking and trying to fool around.

Sure they were right, but they didn't have to make it so hard on us.

As soon as we get there, Maddy goes to the swings and sits down. As she does, she faces away from me, staring into the clear night sky, studying the moon.

I pause, watch as the light from the moon traces her outline, a soft silhouette against the illuminated sky.

"Are you going to push me or not, Ray?"

How could I turn down an invitation like that, eh?

With my first push, I got a chance to feel her back. Sure it was through clothes, but wow, she felt so soft, so warm.

"Not too high now," she says to me. "I don't want to fall off."

"You can't fall off," I says to her. "I won't let you."

At that, her feet stop swinging back and forth to control her motion and she tries to stop herself with her shoes digging into the ground. "A little help," she says.

I held out my hand to grab the chain nearest me. "I'm sorry," I say. "You didn't say you were done."

She looks at me, blushes and with a cold tone in her voice that was so different from her warm glow, she says, "You were just supposed to know, Ray."

And all I wanted to do was get close to her, to find out what first base was all about, so I shut my mouth and nod at everything. "Yes, Madeline. No Madeline. Of course, Madeline."

It all seems so easy when I keep to that script of nodding and going with whatever she wanted to say.

"What's the matter," she says to me after talking about something or another about another girl. "You look sad."

The skin of her hands sent frosty shivers down my spine. "You're awfully cold," I says. "Maybe we should go back."

"Not until you tell me what's going on in your mind," she says.

And the funny thing is, I don't remember much talking about anything. I don't remember saying anything to her about being troubled, but somehow she saw it. She saw everything that was going on in my head like she was some kind of fortune teller or a mind reader or somethin'.

"I don't really want to talk about it," I says. "It's not a good conversation for such a wonderful moment."

"I'll be the judge of that," she says. She tosses her hair over her shoulders and her neck, her beautiful snow-white neck, it lures me in like I want to kiss it. Or bite it.

I was a very confused little boy back then.

"No, seriously, Maddy," I says. "It's not such a good idea."

"Maddy?" she says. Madeline smiles, looks at me and, like she's thinking to herself, says, "I kinda like that."

"I'm sorry," I says. "I was just talking, and that's what came out."

"Maddy is okay with me," she says. "I like it."

"You're not mad?" I ask. "Promise?"

"I'll only be mad if you don't tell me what's bothering you. How are we supposed to be friends if you won't be honest with me?"

That did it. I had to tell her.

And tell her I did. "My mom says that I'm moving, but I don't know where, but I know it's far from here because my dad needs another job. This mine thing ain't working out so well. I guess my dad might get fired, or is going to get fired or something. I don't know. I was too upset to ask questions."

Maddy grasps my hand in hers. Her fingers, each cold as fish, just makes me want to pull back and warm my own hands in my pockets. But I don't. I let her keep them. Even though I was cold, there was something soothing in having another human being touching me. I was sad, but happy at the same time.

Tell you what, I wouldn't ever do that teenager time again. No way, no how. Too confusing, those times.

And when she grasps my hands, she moves her head closer to mine and stares directly into my eyes. "You're not allowed to go anywhere," she says with a smile.

"But I don't know that I have any choice," I says.

"But we just met each other. You aren't allowed to leave me alone so soon."

"I don't even really know how soon it will be."

"And who else will be my boyfriend if you go?"

"Your what?" I says. Everything from my mind shut out at that moment, fled out of my head the way cockroaches scatter when you flick on a light switch. "Boyfriend?"

And she smiles again. This time, with more teeth and glow and everything that I loved about her.

"This is where you're supposed to kiss me, stupid."

My lips did not move. They wouldn't if I moved them with my own hands. So, she did it for me. Her lips met mine.

I tensed up, letting her glossy lips rub over mine. This being the first time I kissed a girl, I naturally have no idea what to expect, so I sit there and let her do all the work.

For what it's worth, girls don't like that, you know. They want you to show some initiative. At least your Maw Maw did.

But everything about this night is so new to me, I thought maybe my heart would explode and destroy my head. Blood and chunks all over the place because that's how little teenage boys imagine their endings.

"You're not really that good at this, are you, Ray?" Maddy wipes her mouth with the back of her hand. "Am I the first girl you've kissed?" she says.

I think my blushing told her everything, because she starts to giggle, hiding it as best she could behind her hands.

"Please," I says. "Please don't tell anyone at school." I grab her hands and force her to look me in the face as I tells her, "You don't understand what it's like to be a guy in high school. I'll be laughed at. Even Tommy will laugh at me," I says. "Please don't let them laugh at me."

"Don't you worry," she says. "I won't say anything."

"Thank you," I says, more like whispering because I'm just catching my breath.

"I won't say anything as long as you stay and be my boyfriend."

And I nodded. I don't know why to this day, I didn't just stop and tell her I couldn't promise nothing. Probably from pure shock. Maybe from not wanting to disappoint her. But mostly from wanting to kiss her again. I may not have been good at it, by God, but I wanted to practice until I was.

After I nod and make that empty promise, Maddy grabs my ears and kisses me again, this time, full on the lips and full force. Ravenous,

I tell you. Like she was hungry.

When I open my eyes from kissing her, I notice the moon hanging over us, nearly three-quarters into the sky above us.

"Maddy," I says. "I think it's best that we get home. I can't keep you out too late on our first date. What will your mom think?"

And at that, Maddy laughs and laughs. "That's not my mother," she says.

That night on the way back to her house, she lets me hold her hand. The humid breeze turned colder somehow while we were at the park, and the rest of the walk back we tried our best to keep each other nearby, feeding off each other's body heat.

"When are we going out again, Ray?" she says.

Stupid me, I says, "I didn't much think about it." Boy did I pay for that one. She slaps me on the arm, nice and hard, then pulls away from me.

"But you're my boyfriend now," she says. "We have to see each other on a regular basis."

These things? These are things you don't know as a fourteen-year-old boy.

"I know that," I says, but lying the whole time. "I was just thinking that maybe we can go see a movie, maybe go to a party or something."

"That sounds really nice," she says. "I'd really like that." She squeezes my hand tighter, sort of like a love hug of my hand.

"Maybe this weekend?" I says. "I got a test in biology that I gotta study for, but after that, I'm all yours."

Maddy smiles and nods, then grasps my hand even harder. "I really hope so, Ray," she says. "I really do." She kisses me on the cheek when we reach the front steps of her house and I watch as she gracefully climbs the stairs to her front door. She blows me a kiss on her soft white hands.

I imagined it fluttering through the air like a butterfly or a moth and landing smack dab on my nose.

All I could do is blush as she goes inside. The first thing I hear, though, when the door closes is "Just why the hell are you late tonight?"

It was a man's voice, probably her dad's, but I couldn't tell. I hadn't met anyone other than that mysterious woman who I thought was her mom but wasn't.

It concerned me at first, to hear so much yelling coming from the house, so I decide to stay by the door and see just how bad things get.

The yelling was normal, I guess. Why are you late? What did you do? Why isn't your room picked up? That type of thing.

What did surprise me were the comments from her that she'd scream back.

I hate you. I hope you die. Why don't you just leave me alone?

As bad as things ever got between me and your grandmaw, I never ever wished she was dead. I just couldn't do that.

But her shouting that stuff back at her own Pa, I figured that she must have known how to take care of herself. If anything, it could help me keep my own head on straight.

I haven't met her father yet—if he even was her father—and I sure as hell didn't want to make a bad impression. Just in case, you know, I end up doing something stupid and have to answer to him.

I wait around till I hear a few doors slam shut and Maddy's frustrated scream into her room. I wanted to go up there, I did, but that would be too far. I had only gone on a first date.

I mean, what if she thought I was too much like a girl, being clingy and worrying. I couldn't do that. Men don't do that, you see. And I was a man.

So, I went home, hoping that maybe we could talk about it later.

If she wanted to bring it up, anyway.

It's on my way home that I notice my friend Billy walking down the sidewalk away from my house.

"Billy!" I shout. "Where were you?" I says.

He looks at me, holds his hands out and screams back, "I was at dinner, where were you? I thought maybe you were in trouble the way Tommy was talking about you."

"No, I'm good." With a smile, I correct that previous statement. "I'm more than good."

"Oh yeah?" says Billy. He's got a coy little smile. "What's so good about tonight?" Then, like a light flashed on in his head. "You had that date with the new girl, didn't you?"

"I don't want to kiss and tell," I says.

"Aw, you dog!" he says and rubs his elbow into mine. "So was it good?" he says. "Is she cute?"

"She's a wonderful kind of gal," I says. "Cute, smart. A little pushy, but that's a woman for ya," I says.

"Welcome to the world of dating," says Billy. He throws his arm around my shoulder and walks me back to my house. "How's it feel?" he says.

"Who am I kidding?" I says. "It feels pretty damned great."

He laughs, rubs my head. "That's my boy," he says. "They grow up so fast. It's true." He pretends to dab a tear out of his eyes. "So what's she like? I trust you'll bring her around some time and let the rest of us meet her?"

"Sure, Billy. Anytime. Just say when and I can bring her around."

"How about, say, tomorrow at lunch?"

Something smelled fishy about the situation, but I let it slide anyway. "Sure, Billy. Tomorrow."

"Good," he says and rubs my head again. "Well, Champ, you're home now. Safe and sound. You have a good night," he says. "Don't let the bed bug bite."

Funny thing is, I knew that Billy musta been up to something, but I couldn't put my finger on it. And as weird as that situation was, I would rather go inside and deal with my pissed off parents than deal with Billy right now. He was just too creepy.

And of course, as soon as I get home, I see my mother standing at the kitchen table, her head in her hands and expressionless, waiting to see what kind of emotion I had.

So, I decided to fuck with her, put on a smile as happy as a clam and waltz right into the kitchen. "Hi, Mom. How's it going?" I get into the cabinets and get myself a drink of water. I play it cool, slick. James Cagney slick as I take a drink of water, look my mom square in the eyes and fake the biggest smile I could possibly imagine.

"Where were you? Your father and I were worried."

"Dad?" I says. "Dad's home?"

"Well, no, not yet he isn't," she says. "He'll be home tomorrow."

"Then how can you say he's upset? He ain't even here!" Again, with a sick, fake smile, I says, "Good night, Mom. Sleep tight."

My mother says nothing to me, instead choosing to watch me go upstairs to my bedroom and close the door.

My clock says it's midnight when my father comes into my room. He tiptoes in, thinking I won't notice him, but it's next to impossible not to. His feet are huge and he steps on everything I have, crunching my clothes into the carpet and making the floorboards creek with agony.

"Son," he says. When he sits on the bed, it's abundantly clear that he's got something up his sleeve. "Son. Ray." His gigantic hand grabs my shoulder and shakes me awake. "Are you awake, Ray?"

"What?" I rub my eyes, but it hurts too much to open them, especially with the hallway light glaring me right in the eyes. Since we moved into that house, I begged for my dad to move it further down the hall so it won't be so bright outside my bedroom door. Each time, they told me it's too hard, too expensive. Yeah, whatever. Next time we need a new oven, they go get one without thinking. "Yes, Dad. I'm awake."

"Your mother says that you gave her some troubles today." My father places both of his hands on his lap and he looks at me, calmly the way a psychologist looks at his patients. "What was that about?"

"Mom says we're moving. I don't want to go."

"And you want your mother to feel bad about you having to move?" he says.

"Well, no, but it's not fair that I have to move." Then, his words finally trickle into my brain. "Wait, what do you mean that I have to move?"

"Well, we're moving when you get out of school, buddy. You'll start school in Charleston."

"First you, now we. What's going on here, Dad?"

My father takes a deep sigh and the baritone in his voice settles to a quiet whisper. He leans in, like he's about to tell me that Santa isn't real again. "Your mother is staying here, in Saraday. You and I, we're going to Charleston. Your mother." My dad takes a deep breath in, then a long, steady pause. "Your mother thinks it's best that she stay here."

"But that doesn't make any sense. Why would Mom decide to stay here and let me leave with you?" A rage of frustration, of not wanting to understand what was really happening, though it trickled into my head in little, leaky drips. "That's just not fair. Why does she get to stay?"

"She thinks it's best," he says. My father grabs the sides of my head and brings it forward to kiss my forehead. "Now go back to sleep. You have school in the morning."

My dad clicked the door shut and let me sleep there, stewing in my own thoughts and fears. When you leave a fourteen-year-old boy alone with his thoughts—especially the bad ones—you give him a can opener for a messy can of worms. I wanted to sleep that night. I really did, but everything I knew, my whole world was getting better and then falling apart on the same day.

So there I am. I can't sleep. I can't even think about going to sleep when I hear something knocking on my window. Being on the second story, I get a little scared at first, but I thought maybe it was Billy or Tommy or something, so I get up and check. Swear to God, I almost messed my pants when I get closer to the window—a rock comes flying at my window, bouncing off the glass right where my nose would be. When I look down, I notice a dark figure. Smaller than Billy and not quite as goofy looking as Tommy, so I open the window.

Hey, I'm up here on the second floor, what's this guy gonna do to me?

I open up the window and dodge another chunk of rock come flying past my head. "What's the matter with you, Billy? Have you lost your marbles?"

"Who's Billy?" It was a girly voice. Not squeaky enough to be Billy or Tommy.

"Maddy? What the hell are you doing here?" I don't realize how loud I am at first, so I stop and turn around, facing the bedroom door. No more lights out in the hallway. Means my dad probably went to sleep. "What's going on?"

Maddy's face looks red, even in the moonlight, and sad. "Can I come up?"

A teenager's daydream and nightmare in one sentence.

"Yeah, sure," I says against my better judgment. "Use that ladder over there."

Maddy looks at me with this statement—a dare, really—that I better not make her climb up a metal ladder meant for clipping tree branches.

"How about you come down here?" she says. "Or maybe we can go somewhere."

"I can't leave again. My dad will kill me."

"Then come down here. I'll wait." And she crosses her arms. "And hurry up. It's cold."

I throw on my house shoes and a shirt and go downstairs while taking slow, light steps. After the stunt I pulled earlier, the last thing I really want to do is anger my parents again.

Not that they don't deserve it, but it wasn't in my heart. I wasn't that kind of kid.

I made it down, no problem, but there's a little bit of an issue. When I make my way downstairs, I have to walk by my parents' bedroom. There, I see my dad sleeping alone. No Mom.

When I go down the steps, I take a look at the living room. Maybe Mom got tired, I think, fell asleep early on the couch and my dad just let her sleep. But when I look into the living room, there's no one there, either.

I try to tell myself to make a mental note of this and bring it up with my dad, but the first priority, I remember, is Maddy.

When I get to the door, I think she sees my shadow through the door's glass window, because I see a shade hop up and down in excitement. "Hurry up," it whispers. "It's getting cold out here."

If I hurry up there, I would wake my dad up, so I had to play this smooth and open the latch nice and slow, lifting the chain to keep it from rattling against the wooden door.

"Will you hurry up, Ray? I'm cold."

I bite my tongue between my molars. I wanna tell her to shut the hell up and let me work this out, but that would just make things worse.

The shade—Maddy—gets closer to the door and as she's just about to peek through the glass, I get the latch completely undone and swing open the door.

And man, she wasn't kidding about it being cold outside. A draft of the wet, cold air gusts up my shorts and gives me goose pimples in all the wrong places. It doesn't help that I'm trying to get Maddy up into my bedroom late at night, too.

I place a hand on my lips to signal for her to be quiet, but she says, "Okay," in her cute Southern Belle accent.

To maybe make a stronger point of it, I take my own index finger and place it against her lips and say, "Shhh."

After she nods in agreement, she follows me upstairs to my bedroom.

"If I would have known you were coming today, I would have cleaned up."

Maddy sits on my bed and removes her coat. The coat has dark stains on the insides of it, near the outside where she buttoned it up.

"What happened?"

"I needed to see you," she says.

"No, no." I point at the dark spots in her jacket. "What happened there?"

"That?" she says. "That's nothing." She takes special care to fold the jacket in half, then half again, to keep the stain out of sight and—she had hoped—out of mind.

"You also have some on your shirt," I says. "Maddy, what happened?"

"You can't tell anyone," she says to me. Her green eyes glow, sparkle like the planets in the sky as she says this. Again, I'm near hypnotized.

"At this point, you're in my room, looking beautiful, and I've got goose pimples all over me. Right now, I will say yes to anything," I says.

She smiles, gives me a kiss on the cheek and whispers, "You're cute" under her breath. "Alright then, but remember. You promised."

I nod and show her my hands to reveal no crossed fingers. "Promise."

"That blood belongs to my parents."

My first reaction: laughter. She's pulling my leg. She has to be. "No, seriously, Maddy. Where's that from? Ketchup?"

"No, it's blood." Her face turns pale against the deep blue of my bedroom walls. "I killed my parents tonight."

"Maddy!" I says with no regard to who will hear me. "You can't kill your parents. You can't stay here. You have to notify the police. Your neighbors. Someone."

"I can't do any of that," she says. "If I do, I go to jail." Maddy leans over my bed and flexes her features so they look straight up at me. "You wouldn't want me to go to jail, would you?"

"Well, no, but you can't just do that. Murdering your parents? You can't get away with this." These words gush out of my mouth before I know my brain is making them. "I mean. You can't. You just." I feel my legs shaking, wanting to give out so I sit down on the bed next to Maddy. "You can't really expect me to just believe that you killed your parents."

"No," she says. Her hands rub the top of my scalp through my hair. "I guess I don't expect you to believe me." As she says this, she grabs her coat and brings it close to her chest and looks at me with these big doe eyes that tell me I'm in trouble no matter what decision I make.

"What are you going to do with the bodies?" I says. "I mean, you just left them there in your house?"

Maddy looks at me and shrugs. "Why not?"

"Are you kidding me?" I says. I grab her by the shirt, by the sleeves and says, "You can't leave dead bodies in your house. If anyone shows up, you're a goner for sure. They'll lock you up right then and there."

"That's if someone comes to my house. No one comes over. Ever." She takes a deep sigh. "You know what the people say about me. About us."

When she says "us," my first thought she meant me and her, but that didn't make immediate sense. Her family was the oddest family in town. Her dad was a control freak, the type of man you know was the nicest in town during the day, but get a drink in him and he'll go to town on his own family and come for yours next.

It wasn't exactly a secret in that town. You just had to know who to talk to.

Some people were more loose-lipped than others, you know?

After some hesitation on her part, I realize that maybe her words have some double meaning. Maybe she means us, too. Me and her. If anyone finds out that she's Madeline Schemel, then I'm fucked. I'll be the guy that dates all the crazies.

"Listen, Maddy, we need to talk this over. I mean, we just had our first date and now you're talking about murdering your parents."

Maddy takes a few steps to her right, covering the distance between my bed and the bedroom door. She says nothing while she smiles at me. Now that I think of it, I bet her parents saw that same smile before they didn't see anything anymore.

"Maddy, what are you asking? Why are you here?" My heart feels like Thumper the Rabbit, knocking around in my chest, trying to come up my throat even. Every swallow I take doesn't even help. Like it's fighting to get out of my chest and run down the street.

"I want you to help me, Ray. I need your help to get rid of the bodies."

"Nuh uh. No way. No how. I can't do that." I put my hands up to keep her away and command some distance between us. "I'm not cut out for that kind of work. You killed them, you deal with it."

"That's not the way this works, Ray." Her face turns paler still, as pale as the moon outside. But there is something weird I notice, something about her eyes and lips. As cold as her face gets, her eyes and lips seem more and more warm. Warm and red like a rose flower. "I need your help."

My eyes itch, then tears fall down and make dark spots on the dark blue carpet. "I can't do that, Maddy. I can't."

"You will," she says.

She blinks, and the colored parts of her eyes, the iris, turns redder and redder until I swear I'm standing at the edge of a pit in Hell.

And that's where I woke up. Before I knows it, I've got a shovel in my hand and I'm digging a ditch with Maddy.

I knows what you're thinking, that it's impossible, but that woman, she was starting to have a helluva effect on me. Whenever she was around, I didn't know if I was really doing what I was doing.

"Dig faster," she says and drops her shovel on the ground. Her face makes no expressions as she turns around and heads into the house. That's right, we're digging in the backyard of her house. She figures that if anyone comes looking, they ain't going to be digging around on her property as long as she could still say no.

I only make it look like I'm digging because I just woke up. I had no ideas what I was actually doing, just moving dirt around mostly. When you come to after passing out, I guess, it's hard to know just where you left off, or what you were doing at all.

So I grab the shovel and pretend that I must have been digging. Far as I could tell, I'm doing something right because she comes out of the house with a smile. Something thuds behind her as she goes down the steps. In the moonlight, I see a reflection off something shiny in her hands.

Shoes. Her old man's shoes. And attached to those, was her old man.

"We're burying them here?" I says. I grab the shovel and carry it like a spear, holding the metal edge between us. "They deserve something better than this."

Maddy's old man thuds on the ground when she lets go of the feet. "That was part of the plan, remember?" she says.

"No, I don't remember anything."

She laughs. That's right, laughs like it's the fucking funniest thing in the world to her. "You're hilarious," she says. She looks down at the hole we're digging, which is barely large enough to hold one of them, let alone a second body. Still, she looks at me and says, "This'll do."

I knows she sees the confusion in my face, but I drop the shovel and stand over the hole. "Um, so what now?"

Maddy drags the body out between us and she says, "Grab a hand."

"Grab a what?"

"A hand." Her head nods toward her old man's hands, scratched up and calloused like he was digging out of something. Closer to my feet is his head.

And as much as I know I didn't do it, I still took a step back.

At least that was my first intention. What I ends up doing is taking a large jump backwards and almost falling on my rear end. "Jesus Christ, Maddy! Where's his eyes?"

Her old man's head had red streaks from his eye sockets down his cheeks. Dried red streaks in thin lines down the sides of his face. In each of his sockets, a dark red, almost black. His left eye looked like it still had something stuck inside, part of an eye or a muscle or something.

"I needed them, Ray. Now stop dilly dallying and grab his eyes."

"I—" I swear to God I felt the burn of my mom's pasta dinner gurgling in my throat, about to come up. "I can't do this."

"Yes, you can, Ray. Grab a fucking hand!" she screams at me. Her voice echoes into the nighttime sky. Like I'm watching the sound move through the neighborhood, I look deeper down the backyards of her neighbors, all the way into the dark sky of the horizon.

No lights coming on. No nosy neighbors.

"No. Fuck this. No." I say. I pick up the shovel back into my hands and start to walk away. I am pretty sure my house is west from here, toward the moon, so I walk in that direction, up Brown Avenue and up to Riverwalk.

"You're not leaving!" she commands.

And my feet, they stop. They stop cold in their tracks. Like I'm stepping in a pit of glue, my feet refuse to move, like they aren't even mine anymore.

"I need to go home," I say.

"No!" she screams.

I'm pulling so hard on my feet that they come clear out of my shoes and I'm free again to run down the street.

"You will stop this instant!" she screams and my body obeys. "Get back here," she says calmer than before.

These are commands she's yelling at me. Commanding to sit, stay. Walk. Grab a shovel. It didn't matter to her, I was some puppet or a pet dog.

No, scratch that. I wasn't her dog. I was lower than a dog. I didn't get no reward. All I got were nightmares about going to jail.

"I didn't want to do this the hard way," she says. Her words feel the velvety smooth like liquid to my brain. "Now grab her hands and help me out."

And just like she commands, I carry out her wishes. Each of my hands grabs one of her old man's. They feel stiff in my grip. Almost like holding wood with a leathery covering.

"Now on three," she says and starts swinging.

"Okay, three and then toss, or do we toss at three?"

"Is this a serious question?"

"Well, yeah, I don't want to hang on to him longer than I have to. If you throw him, then I'm stuck holdin' him and he's just gonna fly my way."

"No, he will not."

"So three and toss, or three then toss?"

Maddy's reflect red moonlight. Then, after a second or two, she says, "Three and then toss."

"Okay. Three, then toss."

"Wait, wait, wait," she says and then drops the feet at her side. "I need to do something first."

"Do what?" I says. My hands won't release her old man's wrists, like glued to them or something.

"This," she says and picks up the shovel, brandishing it at me.

"You're going to kill me?" I says.

"No, pffsht." She looks at me, then down at her old man's corpse. "Of course not. I still need you."

And I'm not sure if that's a compliment or an insult, but I try to take it at face value. "Right, right."

"So, then what are you doing with that shovel?" I says.

Maddy takes the shovel in both hands and holds the metal part down, standing over her old man's body. "Just a second," she says. "I need to concentrate."

Then, looking down at her old man, she says some words to herself in secret, mumbling something like in Spanish or French or something. I didn't take any of those languages, so I didn't know what she might have been saying.

I would have asked, but things was already quite intense at that moment. It just didn't seem the right time.

And not like it would have made any difference. Seemed to me like everything was at least a little weird that night.

When she finished mumbling, though, she opened her eyes, looked down then closed them tight.

She mumbles, "Mors tua, vita mea," and then brought the shovel clear through the old man's throat with a sound like someone slammed a pound of raw hamburger meat on the counter.

When I look down to see what just tapped at my shoe, there's the man's open mouth, his front teeth gripping the toes of my shoe.

9

POP POP

I can't even look at her at school the next day. I can't explain what happened, and the more I think about it, the less I want to explain it.

So I carefully plan out my day on the way to school. Avoid every hallway I know she's going to be down. Keep my head down, style my hair a little different than usual, you know, to stay hiding in plain sight.

It works for about half the day, until lunch time.

When I take a quick glance at the usual table, you know, to make sure Billy and Tommy are already there, I see Maddy's big auburn hair just waiting for me to sit down next to her. Her bright green eyes are searchlights, scanning the room for me. Ready to arm her guns and go in for the kill.

At least that's how it felt. I mean, how do you explain that you ain't got a girlfriend no more because you had to help bury her parents in the backyard?

It just ain't something that's supposed to be said, much less thought about. And I couldn't help it all day, thinking about it.

No joke, I rehearsed it to myself in the middle of math and history classes. Couldn't pay attention to none of the lectures, and probably failed my history test. I was so out of it, I probably wrote my explanation and break up speeches for the essays. Wouldn't surprise me none.

But I was stuck there without no escape plan. She was at our table, and soon Tommy and Billy would be there, too. I couldn't let them down.

I could maybe pretend to be sick, maybe let the nurse try to send me home. But honest, I doubt it would be the great escape I hoped for. I'd have to deal with that creepy girl sooner or later.

My heart does this beating in my throat thing again, so I swallow it down, hold my breath, and take a step toward the table. I stop when I feel the burning of her eyes searing into my skin.

"Ray!" she shouts. If people didn't suspect that maybe we'd be dating then, they sure as hell were now.

Put on a fake smile, wave for the show. "Hi, Maddy!" I says. I'm clutching my brown bag lunch so tight I think I might tear holes through the paper. But I sit down anyway and smile. "How are you?" I says.

She nods and looks into my eyes. I mean, deep, deep into my eyes, like she's looking for signs of betrayal. I wanna tell her that I didn't say nothing to nobody, but I don't know who'd hear me if I did say something. For a stupid fourteen-year-old, I could be pretty smart sometimes.

"I'm great," she says. "Got your lunch?"

"Yeah, brown bagging it today. Mom made me a sandwich." I feel tempted to take it out and show it to her, like I'm somehow guilty of lying to her about my sandwich, too.

I know I didn't do nothing, but it's this type of pressure that I swear was gonna kill me one day, let me tell you.

But Maddy says nothing about my sandwich, like she didn't even care. She smiles at me and looks away. Coy like a girl does when she's mad at you and don't know why.

"Would you like some?" I ask. I told the sandwich in both of my hands, ready to tear it apart at a moment's notice if I had to. All I was waiting for was the word.

"No, no," she says. "I'm fine."

And it's funny, but I don't believe when she says this to me. "No, really," I says. "I insist."

My fingers grip tight onto the sandwich and I tear it into two pieces, mostly uneven because the ketchup made the bread slippery, but it was even enough for us both to have a good size piece.

"Ray, I'm good, thank you." She sticks her hand out, pushing my sandwich back toward me.

"Suit yourself," I say and take a bite out of the sandwich. "More for me."

"Don't talk with your mouth full, Ray. Didn't your mother teach you any manners?"

How women can get away with saying whatever they want while men feel guilty for even thinking bad thoughts, I don't know how. It's unfair, but my fourteen-year-old self didn't know that then.

"Actually, she taught me to praise the chef whenever I felt like it," I says. "After all, she was the chef." I sit there with a shit-eating grin, happy as a gaddam clam at my wise ass self.

"Cute, Ray. Now I can see your sandwich." She crosses her arms across her chest. "That ham looks disgusting."

"Ha!" I says. "You couldn't see anything!" I point my finger in her face, so close she could bite it off. "It's not ham, it's turkey!"

"What do we have here?" says Billy, sitting down with his sandwich. "Some love birds came to roost?"

Tommy follows after him and sits down, grinning like he knows something I don't.

"We're not lovebirds, Billy," I says and immediately know I'll pay for that one later. "We're just sitting down waiting for you."

"You look tired, Ray. What were you doing last night?" says Billy. He smiles, coy like, while chewing his sandwich and munching on some celery sticks his mother must have given him.

"I was up late, reading. That's all."

"You look tired, too, miss," says Billy, nodding at Maddy.

"You can keep wondering why, you jerk."

Billy's smile goes turns upside down fast and Tommy laughs, literally slapping himself on the knee. "Gee, ma'am, I didn't mean anything by it," he says, but winks at me.

"Billy," I says. "This is Madeline. Madeline, this is Billy."

Billy extends his hand across the table to grasp Maddy's, but she looks at him with a cold stare instead. "I'm not touching that," she says. "Nice to meet you."

Billy nods. "Nice to meet you, too."

"Hi, Maddy," Tommy says. He damn near throws his hand across the table and knocking over our bottles of soda with his elbow.

Maddy shows him up, though. "I'm not touching that, either."

"Say, you look familiar, Madeline. You sure you're new here?"

"Billy, give it a rest, will ya?" I rest my hand on Maddy's hands, folded together.

She looks around to not see Billy in the eyes, when she says, "Yes, Billy, I'm new here."

"Is that so?" he says. "Really?" He takes a bite out of his sandwich, chews it a time, then a second time and swallows the whole bite. One gulp. "Cuz that's not what Tommy says here."

Fuck this. Fuck them both, I says to myself. "Billy, you don't know what you're talking about."

"Sure I do," he says. "Don't I Tommy?"

"Billy, what are you doing?" says Tommy. His eyes turn shifty, not wanting to look at anyone straight away. "I don't know nothing."

"That's bullshit and you know it, Tommy. Tell Ray and Madeline what you told me. Tell us what Ray told you."

Maddy's eyes turn to me, her green eyes probably turning a Christmas tree light red, blinking her spells on me. "What did you tell him, Ray?"

"Nothing," I says. "I said nothing."

"You're lying to me," she says.

"You tell him, ma'am," says Billy.

"Will you just shut the hell up?" I says. My feet search underneath the table to kick Billy in the shins, but the smart aleck hides them under his chair.

"Shut up, Billy," I says.

"Yes, Billy," says Maddy. "I'm sure he can answer for himself." My eyes blur, dizzy kind of blur. A fire burns deep inside my head.

"Nothing, I swear. It wasn't anything big."

"Was it nothing or nothing big?" she says. "Which was it, Ray?"

I know what she's thinking. Her new invention risks being blown wide open if anyone else finds out about her being a Schemel, a nothing. A nobody.

"Nothing, it was nothing big."

"You're doing it again," she says. "Just tell us. What did you tell them?"

And no matter what I do, I'm in trouble. So, I go for broke: "I just said your last name, that's it."

"You what?" says Maddy, like she really didn't see this coming.

"That's my boy," says Billy. He extends his hand across the table, nearly elbowing me in the face. He says, "Hi, Madeline Schemel. I'm Billy Barnes, I believe we've met before last year in Chemistry."

"Go to Hell," she says. She gets up, but as she does, her eyes don't leave my forehead. Like screwdrivers, drilling into my skull, digging deeper and deeper. Searing my brain.

"Ray? You don't look so good," says Tommy. "You need some water or something?"

"Yeah, Tommy, I'm good."

"Need water or something?"

"Maybe some water, Tommy. Maybe that sounds nice," I says.

"What's the matter, Ray?" she says. "You do look kinda pale."

And I'm thinking this bitch knows exactly what's happening. It's all bullshit. But I say nothing. I can't afford to say nothing because I can't prove that she's doing anything to me.

But she has to be. She's gotta be.

"Just a headache. I swear." I grip the sides of my head and rub, pressing my fingertips into my temples like I'm searching for a magic button, something to shut my brain off. "Just a headache."

"Are you sure it ain't nothing," she says.

"Don't be like that, okay?" I says. "Don't be like that."

"Just you wait when everyone hears about how hot you got, Schemel," says Billy. He covers his mouth to hide his surprise. He knows how offensive it is to be so happy about someone's secret getting out. Can't nobody start over in the Land of Opportunity anymore?

"Here's your water, Ray," Tommy says. He offers a paper cup into my hands. "Sorry I took so long, there was a line for the water fountain."

"It's fine," I says, take a sip of the water. It cools my throat but does nothing for my head. "Thanks, Tommy."

Tommy's eyes smile at the compliment.

"Just you wait and see what everyone says, Madeline. I mean, it's like that story, 'Ugly Duckling'," says Billy. "You know?"

He gets up from the table and tucks his button down back into his pants and wanders to the closest group of boys and girls. While staring right at me and Maddy, he leans in and whispers something to them.

"Why the hell did you tell him that?" Maddy throws her bag at me before we even reach the doors outside.

"It just slipped," I tells her. "I swear."

"I'm sure it was. Just a slip." Maddy throws herself at me, but her hands rattle the lockers next to my ears, shaking the wall I'm leaning up against. "Do you know what I admired the most about you?"

I shook my head.

"It was your daring, your ability to take a chance. I didn't think you'd dare risking all of that by making me another pariah."

"I did no such thing," I says, not knowing what the hell any pariah is. I'd ask, but I think I'd prove her point.

"You really are that stupid, aren't you?," she says. "You're an idiot, Ray Thurman. A liar and an idiot."

"It just came out!" I shout as she walks away, grabbing her bag and slinging it over her shoulder. With each step, her hips rise and fall, smooth and sexy like waves of an ocean. "I never meant to say anything to him."

"And you will regret it," she says, not looking back, but shouting it into the air. "You'll regret every second of it."

10

POP POP

My head became my world that evening when I went home. When you risk having a screaming fire rush through your head in a wave of massive heat, you watch everything you do that might trigger it.

Anything I could have done might could piss off Maddy. I never knew when she was watching, maybe watching right then, look at me and make me cry in pain.

Maybe she'll do it cuz I scratched my ass, played with my balls. I didn't know and it scared the hell out of me.

I couldn't tell your great grandmaw, your great grandpop. It seemed like a weird thing. Maybe they'd take me to Dr. Strong, maybe get me some kind of medication.

Truth, if it would have helped, I think I would do it. But it wouldn't. I knew that then.

So what do you do when the craziest woman in the world is out to get you? You read.

At least that's what I do. I grabbed the latest Hardy Boys book and curled up on my bed, hoping to get through the whodunit as fast as I could until it was time to go to bed.

You know that feeling when you're in a hurry to go to sleep because you're so bored? That's me, reading and going over words, reading the same phrases, words, syllables over and over again.

"Hey, sport, how was school today?" This precedes my dad coming into the room and sitting down on the bed next to my feet. His strong jaw and cold blue eyes watch me turn the page. Page after page.

"It was okay," I says. Glance over more words, turn the page.

"Just okay?" he says. Pop shoves himself backwards as far as he can go until his back is against the bedroom wall.

"Just okay," I says. Turn the page. See--but not read--more words. An awkward silence rings loud in my ears. If I couldn't read before, I sure as fuck can't do it now.

"So, um," Pop says. "Do you have any, you know, special ladies?" Pop nudges at my foot with a closed fist. "Well?"

I feel the heat of embarrassment blanket my face.

"You do, don't you?"

"There might be a girl," I says. "Maybe."

"Just maybe?" he says.

"How's Mom?" I says.

Pop taps my foot with his hand and stands up. He adjusts his tie, pulling it higher on up to his neck. "Good talk," he says. "Enjoy your book."

When the door shuts, I turn the page and listen for footsteps.

True to their nature, the floorboards squeal in pain from my dad's heavy feet. I wait until the sound turns faded, turns round the corner and down the steps.

Opening the window, I feel the first breeze grab my attention as it slips against my skin. My arms turn into tiny bumps--goose pimples. I don't even think to grab a jacket. It seems like too much weight and too many details to pay attention to.

With the ladder still by the window thanks to my parents' inattentive natures--thank you fighting mom and pops--I slip down the ladder and run toward Maddy's house.

"There's a chance," I tell myself, alone in the brisk spring air. "There's a chance."

The skin on my feet touch every rock, every nugget of broken cement. They rush forward, half rolling, half running, few blocks to Maddy's house. With the exception of my wanting to keep Maddy happy and not have her want to fry my brain, it's a pretty nice night. Perfect weather, bright moon.

It feels peaceful for the first time in a long time.

And that's what disturbs me, so I run faster.

At the front door, I can't knock. My hand gets only inches from the wood, almost touching paint. But I can't. I can't touch that damn door.

That feeling, of having Maddy tell me what to do, that's the same feeling I git when trying to touch that door with my knuckles. "Maddy!" I shout. "Maddy, dammit, get down here!"

Only one light comes on, the light from what I guess is her bedroom.

"Maddy!"

Something goes off in my head. A switch, like someone cut a rubber band off my brain.

I tap on the door, meeting my knuckles to the painted wood. "Maddy?"

When the generous door decides to open and allow me into the house, no one welcomes me.

"Hello?" I says. "Maddy?" My hand searches for the door while my eyes poke and pry every corner down the hallway for a shadow, a person, anything that tells me that this whole scene ain't as creepy as it seems.

I grip the door, feeling the chipped paint panels of the door with my fingertips, shoving it back on the hinges. The slam echoes down the hallway.

Someone will surely hear that, I think to myself. She can't ignore me now.

"Maddy?" I calls out. "Maddy!"

But still, that woman ain't listening to a word I says. So, since the door decided to open, I goes ahead and let myself in.

The house smells like dust with a faint maroon glow that taints the color of everything in every room. The furniture looks plush and hold. Some kind of red wood frames the arms of the couch and chairs placed neat and perfect on the edge of a fancy gold and green carpet. The only source of light comes from an electric lamp that looks like a candelabra.

The lamp even flickers like real lamps, so shadows and shades of things dance against the walls, but only in the corner of my eyes.

The most logical place to start, I decides, is the upstairs. I'm thinking that maybe she's hiding up there. If I can find her, I can explain everything and maybe not worry about having her start a bonfire in my brain.

I rub my eyes when they start to twitch. Maybe paranoia, maybe warning me. "It's not Maddy," I say. "It's not Maddy."

Just because I'm paranoid doesn't mean she ain't out to get me.

"Maddy?" I whisper.

My feet bump into the edge of the stairs. I lean forward, only holding myself up with one hand against the wall. "Maddy?" I say.

It goes against every sane bone in my body to go upstairs, but I do it anyhow. My first step announces my intentions as the stairs groan.

"Maddy," I say, not whispering or nothing, just talking like normal. "Maddy, I'm coming up. I want to talk to you."

I can feel the dead silence in my bones. Chilly cold like a layer of snow on my skin. It's way too quiet for anyone to still be here. And while I'm only halfway up the stairs, I start to think that I should maybe go back home, tuck myself back in bed and warm up my feet.

"Maddy," I shout. The sound of my voice bounces off the pictures on the wall, rattling their dark wooden frames against the faux wooden paneling.

"Maddy?" I say one more time. My next step reaches the top of the stairs and I pause, turning my head just a little bit to listen for clues if Maddy was there.

I go in small steps down the short, short hallway, maybe twelve feet long, if that. The doors on the right and left sides of the hall are all closed, leading to bedrooms, I think.

I open the door to the one I think is Maddy's and let the door swing open. It only goes halfway, but it's enough for me to see a pink bedroom, white walls and a lamp lit on a desk by the window. Papers and pens and pencils lie scattered across the desk, looking like something of an artist's work desk.

I search the desk for drawings, signs of craziness. A few scratches here. A homework assignment there. Nothing serious and no clues.

Well, no clues but a stench that creeps into my nose when I turn away from the desk.

The smell begs me to seek it out. The sweet floral scent mixed with putrid rot of something once living. The smell pours from under the closet door. Must be a strong scent to rush out in such strength from a small opening.

Against my better judgment, I open the door. Slowly at first, until I feel confident that nothing will jump out at me. What I see—well—what I see causes me to burp acid into my mouth. The smell turns my stomach, churning my food around and around. Moving the clothes to get a better view, I see a small altar. A metal five-pointed star lies on the middle of a small table covered with a black cloth. The cloth has gold stars stitched into them. A white and a yellow taper candle, melted halfway down sit in glass holders at each of the far corners.

In a black metal bowl, something the size of a cereal bowl, sat two red and white balls. A fly landed on one of them, buzzing and prancing about the surface until it disappears into the bowl.

These are eyes. Brown eyes, staring at each other in the bowl.

I can't keep the acid down much longer, and I feel the rush of burning stomach acid pour into my mouth and leak out through the corner of my lips.

The smell burns the back of my throat and tastes like the insides of my nose when I get a cold around Thanksgiving time. I can't help the vomit landing on the linoleum floor of the closet, but try to stifle the leak with the back of my hand. Maybe hold it back a little.

I need to go home, so I turn around. The words, "Should I or shouldn't I swallow?" roll around in my head the way a basketball rolls on a junior high gym court. My tongue shuffles the mucous goo from cheek to cheek. If I think about cotton candy, it doesn't taste so damn bad.

My hand pushes in each of the doors as I leave the hallway and take slow, careful steps downstairs.

The closest bathroom is downstairs, I find, next to the living room.

My foot closes the door behind me. I lean over the sink and open my mouth. The red-green liquid leaves my mouth and splatters the sides. Out of courtesy, I take the risk of making noise and turn on the faucet to wash down the goo.

My pants serve as a good towel as any, and with careful footing, I step out of the bathroom and search the downstairs and living room for any signs of life. As before—none.

As I walk to the door, I think about the bodies buried outside in graves I helped to dig. It sends a chilly rumble down my arms and legs, more goose pimples and a tinge of regret.

Then, there's this feeling, a feeling that I'm being watched, or maybe hunted. They say you can feel the stares of other people on the back of your neck.

It's true, I tells ya. Totally true.

When I turn around, there's not much more than a coat rack and a couch.

This is my cue, I think, to just bust my hump and get going home. My parents might find out I am awake, maybe they'll ground me.

Good, I think for a minute. I'll be safe from her.

The door opens almost by itself again, letting me get outside and once again into the chill of the springtime night air. The walk back home goes by faster than I hoped it would and I climb back to my bed. The sheets feel so hot against the chill in my toes that I go immediately numb, then warm. It's about fifteen seconds before I feel my toes move when I flex.

I want to sleep, but the darkness in the window, the lights from the sky, the images of that altar, everything hangs as unwanted ghosts.

Then, speaking of unwanted ghosts, I get up and figure, if she finds out I've been in her house, Maddy will kill me for sure. So opening my window, I peek out from side to side outside my window and push the ladder out and down to the ground.

The metal rattles, making enough noise to make dogs bark across the street.

Screw the dogs, I just hope I can make it into my bed before the lights come on in the hallway.

In bed, I do this trick that I learned when I was little and wanted to catch the tooth fairy red-handed. I lay down, close my eyes and push my head into the pillow, just slightly downward so it's harder for my mom or dad to see what I'm doing.

My dad flicks on the hallway light. A bright yellow beam lights up the underside of my door and I watch as feet scuffle along the carpet, but stops first at my door.

The door cracks open, but no head pops in. I open my own eyes, watch the goings on as my dad closes the door and steps downstairs. Each step creaks louder than the next until he's finally downstairs and opens up the door.

He doesn't see me, but I'm watching my dad say, "What the hell?" while standing just below my second story window.

11

POP POP

Some warm water and a thermometer on a light bulb for a few seconds tells my Ma that I should maybe stay home the next day.

She kisses me on the forehead and tells me to drink plenty of fluids and get lots of rest.

After last night, the last thing I want is to get to school, have Maddy think something's up, and let me get in trouble. So I stay still in bed and read until I fall asleep. Then I wake up, make me a sandwich, and fall asleep again. You know, actin' like I was sick, but not really being sick.

This plan backfires, however, when Maddy shows up after school.

The one thing I didn't expect that crazy broad to do.

"Ray!" she says. "You're home!"

Maddy carries her backpack into the kitchen and leaves it on the table.

"You'll mess up the decorations, Maddy," I tells her and put the backpack on the ground.

"But I want it up here," she says and raises the bag again. "You don't mind, do you?" Her eyes burn into mine, like some psychotic connection or something. Her brain to mine.

"No, it's fine," I says. My hands take her backpack and rests it on the table. "See? No harm."

"I'm terribly thirsty," she says. "Water?"

I don't ask how much, ice or not. It's like the instructions are already in my brain. Two ice cubes, water out of a pitcher, not the tap. A napkin to collect the droplets on the outside of the glass.

She drinks the water and smiles at me. All I see, however, are her features. They jiggle as she laughs at herself--something about her throat feeling cold--and then she snaps her fingers. My eyes shoot straight to hers. Another connection locked and loaded.

"What's wrong, Ray?" she says. "Sick?"

Two coughs into my fist get my throat nice and scratchy--or scratchier--and I says, "Yeah, cold or something. Felt something in my throat." Cough again for emphasis like a punctuation mark.

"Aww," she says and hands me the glass. "You should drink this, then." Her hands offer it to me, her face cocks to the side and her eyes shine bright as green stars. "Help to keep you from being dry," she says. "Or honey will do, too." She winks. "Old family secret." She presses her index finger against her mouth and whispers, "Shhh, don't tell anyone." Her lips form a heart shape as she says this. Swear to God.

"Yeah, thanks for that," I says. "What brings you here?" Cough.

"Making sure you were okay," she says. "I got a little worried. There were a lot of people out today. Said something big was going around."

"Who else was out?" I says. My timing couldn't have been that good, I think.

She looks at me and winks. Strangest thing. She says, "You shouldn't go thinking those things."

I can't help but swallow quickly. "What things?"

"You want to kill me," she says with a smile. A damned smile, James. Accusing me with a smile.

"I wasn't thinking nothing."

She taps her forehead and nods. "And that's a lie, too."

"No, it's not." I sit back on my bed, scooting backwards. I know I'm a trapped rat. "Honest."

"You know," she says, "Tommy was out. Rumor has it, his mom didn't even say anything to the school."

"No kidding?" I says. "Tommy, too?"

Maddy nods and looks at me. "You have Mrs. Jonas for English?" she says. Her hands fling her backpack over her shoulder, her eyes remain locked on mine. "Our homework is reading act three of Romeo and Juliet. Don't forget." Her smile sends me instant chills down my shoulders to my feet. When I see her, I see those eyeballs in a bowl. Her candles. The bodies buried out in her backyard.

"Thanks, Maddy," I says. "I should be okay to go to school tomorrow."

"Good," she says. Her smile terrifies the hell out of me. "You look better already."

She blows me a kiss and lets herself out the door.

When she leaves, I get dressed as fast as I can and run to Tommy's. If he's been sick, too, I want to try the same trick Maddy used. Tell him his homework and see if he's okay.

When I get to the front door, there's a man in a dark suit sitting on the steps. He's smoking a cigarette, looking into the smoke, lost in whatever images he's viewing.

The man puts his hand out to me and shakes his head. "Tommy

can't see you now," he says. His voice was raspy and dark.

So I didn't bother to fight with the man. He was angry, it looked like. But sad at the same time.

And he wasn't Tommy's dad. But some other guy. He looked official. Like a secret service agent or somebody. But not that I would know, you see. I was only fourteen. Hardly enough to know who was who in the real world. Hard to know what was happening.

After that, I run to Maddy's house. I didn't want to, but I felt like I had to.

On the way there, I stop and grab a rock. A solid, sharp rock.

Maddy did this to him. I didn't have any proof. Couldn't accuse her in a court of law, boy, but she did something.

Maybe like those burning eyes.

And so I get the rock and hide it in my pocket.

When I get to the door, I knock and Maddy answers almost before I can grab the rock in my pocket.

"Hi," she says. "Fancy meeting you here."

"Tommy," I say.

She nods. The girl knew what I was thinking. What I was talking about.

I saw red, my muscles tensed up.

After that, I remember my body moving, and it was like me watching myself.

Like when I dug up those holes and helped to bury those bodies.

I swing the rock at her face. For a brief second, I feel the drag of the rock's edge against her skin.

I pause in surprise.

She pulls back and grabs her face.

After that, I woke up somewhere in the park. A knife in shoulder and a message on my forearm.

12

JAMES

"What did you do then?" I ask Pop Pop. "What did the message say?" He stares into the wall of his room like he's lost in thought, then pulls down his sleeve. His lower lip looks wet, slick with memories. It actually quivers for a bit. "Pop Pop?" I ask, just a bit louder.

He snaps back and comes to. His eyes dilate as he looks at me and through me and into me all at the same time.

"Then nothing," he says. "Ferget I said anything at all." He waves for me to leave the room. "You should get home now."

When I take a peek at his arm, Pop Pop hides it by sliding his left forearm off the rail of his chair, pretending to grab his wheel. He's had a tattoo there for years. A butterfly, of all things.

I asked him once, why he got it.

"To remind me that beautiful things can happen," he told me.

And that was that.

It never occurred to me that he'd be covering something up.

"But Pop Pop, what happened to Tommy and Billy?"

"Tommy died," he says. He sounds angry. The word 'died' with a hard, crisp sound. He might as well have said "tied."

"I'm sorry, Pop Pop."

"It was ages ago," he says. He wheels himself around, facing the doorway. "You spend too much time digging up old shit," he says.

"I'm a reporter," I tell him. "You should know that's what we do."

"You could have gone into the army or something. Did something different. More masculine with your life. This running around and writing stuff up, this creepy shit that no one wants to talk about. It does nothing to better the future of the American people."

"Is that why you remember every single little detail about her, Pop Pop? Because you don't care?"

He turns his head away from me, staring at the wall again. Like he sees something—maybe her—deep inside it.

"That's not what I said," he says.

"Please, tell me. What else happened?" The lights in the hallway light up enough that we can see heavy and dark shadows cast along the floor. Pop Pop's shadow throws a big enough shade on the walls that I can barely make out what used to be on there. The heavy shadow appears thick. Almost like I could scoop it up with a spoon. Right off the wall.

"You need to go," says Pop Pop. "I'm late for my dinner."

"You're not late," I say. "It's barely five o'clock."

"I'm old. I eat early," he says. He wheels himself out.

13

POP POP

The boy didn't have to know shit. He knew well enough this was nothing for him to be messing with.

He didn't need to fear no mirrors.

She wasn't after him.

She was after me. But I ain't telling the boy that.

He looked like me, blessed with my handsome good looks and his mother's brains. Not a bad balance, if I say so.

But James leaves the room, leaving me to myself.

The photo that he brought with him, stuck in a cheap frame that I bought to keep it from getting dirty and destroyed.

The frame gives it more credit than I want to, though. No need to fake any sentimentality about that photo.

The parts I left out?

That photo was taken at our first date. My mom insisted we take more pictures. This was after she had told me we were moving, so she got kinda sentimental. I think she figured I would be, too.

I told it to him because, well, I don't remember it. Not much, anyhows.

I remembers going to the park and hanging out. I remember swinging on the swings, I remember the dark sky, sparking like the moon on the lake in the distance.

I remember her, in a pink dress. She looked different that night. Older, I guess.

I thought maybe at first it was the makeup. But it wasn't.

That strange Spanish or Italian mumbo-jumbo, that's what it was.

But we were on the swings. These ones screeched out because of the rusted chains that held those hard, black plastic seats in place. I pushed Maddy on the swingset, standing a good distance behind her.

I remember she was barefoot. Her shoes, nice shiny black slippers were off to the left of the swingset, out of the sand.

As I push her, I notice a little bit of drag of her toes in the sand.

"Stop," she says to me.

I can't help myself but to listen, so I listen. She slows herself down, then steps up from the sitting position smooth and effortlessly like a ghost. I swear, I almost never saw her feet move.

Something seemed to be messing around in the bushes, so she creeps up there in her barefeet.

"Maddy," I whisper. "Whatcha doing?"

And I knew I was supposed to be the man, go up there, and protect her from whatever was lurking in those bushes. But I couldn't move. Not an inch.

She raised her arm out to her side, then bended her elbow to tell me to stop what I'm doing.

Of course, I obeyed. Like watching myself on a movie. I was whipped like a dog.

Maddy leaned down onto the ground, not caring that her dress was getting wet and grass stains.

When I felt my feet were free, I nudged along. I took small steps, though. I didn't want to get caught up in whatever might be happening out there.

But something came out. Something small. Something furry.

It squeaked, its little nose twitching as it sniffed Maddy. I must've liked her. It walked up to her, like she was Cinderella or something.

Maddy looked at me over her shoulder, smiling. And that smile made me feel warm inside, so I smiled back.

"Come here," she said.

I followed her, slowly, up to the squirrel.

"What are you going to do?" I asked.

"I need this," she says to me. She waves her hand over the head of the squirrel, and the damned thing just sat down. It sat down and stared at her.

"Can you do dogs, too," I asked. But she don't get the joke.

Her fingers crawled like spiders on the grass until she can reach out and grab the squirrel around the belly and sides. She pulled him closer out to her chest and she seemed to be whispering to it.

And the words were slow, steady, and familiar.

"Vita mea," she whispered.

Then, quickly, she grabbed the squirrel's head, snapped it clean off, and poured the blood on the ground.

I took a step back, but I felt myself being pulled toward her.

I wanted to throw up. I remembered that snap. Never ferget it. Like that crisp snap and pop that happens when you open a soda bottle. Every damn time, I think about that squirrel.

And the blood poured in a thick, dark pool on the grass.

I don't remember much after that.

But I remember thinking, as we walked up Main Street, that she looked beautiful. She was gorgeous, and somehow lost the makeup she had on before.

That night I don't remember if we kissed.

I don't remember if what happened to that squirrel's body. I don't remember shit.

I do remember the nightmares. Not specifics. But blood. Bats. Darknesses. Being tied up and having Maddy dance around me.

That boy of my daughter's. He thinks he knows fear. He thinks he knows what it's like to stare out your windows after you move. Wondering if she's out to get you.

But it's his now. His cross to bear. And I ain't telling him anything. Let him suffer. Let him find out what it takes to survive.

14

JAMES

No less than a dozen animal heads watch as I wait for my second drink for the day. The animals have those frightening glass eyes, dead and lifeless. Yet, they watch me watch them. And it might be the first shot of well whiskey talking, but I think the bobcat is smiling at me.

One of four bars in the small town of Saraday, Barry's is the oldest and darkest. Which is why I'm sitting here at twelve noon, trying to not stare into the mirror behind the bar. To compensate, my eyes wander the dark wood paneling of the walls and stained wooden floors. The smell's not bad if you like Lysol and the sweet and sour smell of fermented vomit.

The bartender, Barry's great-grandson Allen, hides out in the back. This bar used to have a kitchen but due to a small fire ten years ago, Allen made the executive decision: alcohol plus fire equals potential property damage.

If he's really concerned about fire damage, he should have unplugged that broken jukebox with the frayed wires years ago.

A girl sits to the left of me at the bar. She's wearing a dark blue skirt that comes down to her knees and sandals that wrap around her leg up to her calf muscles. Her blouse is white, nothing fancy except what looks like tiny bird wings on her chest.

She runs her hands over the bottle to caress it, to feel the cold in her palms. Her fingers leave wet smudges on the brown glass that disrupts the path of dripping condensation. This girl's head drops forward. Her eyes seem to focus on the base of the bottle. Or the wet ring it left on the counter. From this far away and in this lighting, who can really tell. Maybe she's just wasted to hell.

"What?" she says. I watch her mouth move in the gigantic mirror before us. My chest feels tight, staring off into the mirror. My hands shake. Feet twitch.

I resist the urge to close my eyes, to pull back and throw myself under the bar. Instead, I remember my therapist's words. "Count to three. There is no danger. No woman in the mirror."

The girl's eyes wander toward me. She looks concerned, not wanting to lock eyes.

My eyes gravitate to the mirror again. The girl, her lips make smaller movements. Whoever she's talking to, she doesn't want me to hear.

I see myself in the mirror. I don't mean to, seriously I don't, but I like to check over my shoulders.

Nothing's there, but I can't help but to smile. The mirror reflects both of us at the counter, making the both of us look twice as drunk.

The wooden slab underneath my ass swerves in the same direction as my head when I look her directly in the eyes. Her sunglasses covered much of her retinas so she had to look over the brims to see. I tell her, "Have you seen Allen anywhere?" She takes the glasses off and rests them on her head just above her hairline. Her gray hair hangs loose over her temples and ears. She looks like she might have just gotten out of bed. Maybe just woke up here. Bags the size of airplane luggage hang just under each of her eye sockets.

"My apologies," I tell her. "I thought you were a local. Allen is the bartender."

A solemn sigh escapes her lips. She nods and mutters, "I know."

"There should be a statute of limitations on punishments," I tell her and hold up my empty glass. "I ordered a drink thirty minutes ago." The glass makes a heavy clink against the countertop. "Maybe I should have tipped an extra dollar."

She nods and the bottle meets her lips for a drink.

"You know today is my first day of freedom," I say.

Still no response.

"They ought to stop hounding you for everything that you've done," I say.

"You are preaching to the choir," she says finally. "I've taken on a full time job so I could escape this town. Been trying to leave all my life," she says.

This girl next to me, she sits up a little bit and adjusts her glasses again. The sun shines through the windows, a flashlight from God.

"It's the anniversary," I say. "I'm allowed to drink," I mutter as I stare out at the open street outside. The bar isn't dingy in the sense of dirt, but it's not the type of place that anyone visits at noon in the morning.

"Me, too," she says. Her lips almost smile. "You're married?"

"Nope. Never married," I say and take another drink. "Last day of therapy."

"That's wonderful," she says. "Congrats."

I scoot over to sit next to this woman. "Nice to meet you, ma'am," I say. "My name is James."

"Emma," she says. Her hand feels soft, manicured. "My husband bought me a stuffed animal for our last anniversary. It was a stuffed dog that said 'I love you' when you squeeze it."

"That's not so bad," I say.

Her smile reveals an inch long scar on her chin. The wrinkled skin pulls tightly on her cheek and neck as she speaks to me.

"My husband became the father I never had," she says. "That father figure that you always saw with your friends but never yourself. The one who punished accordin' to the law and, mind you, his word was law."

"Ouch," I say and whistle. I offer my empty glass out to her to cheers, but her eyes stay fixed on the brown glass of the bottle.

Someone from the outside opens that door, letting in God's flashlight. When the door closes, he stops for a minute to adjust his eyes.

"Another sinner," I say.

"In that Catholic kind of way, haven't we all sinned?" she says. Her voice droops like a loose-fitting curtain on a window.

"Some more than others, I guess."

"How so?" she says.

"I doubt we have the time," I say between slurps.

My friend, her eyes fix to the wall clock above the bartender. "We've got about a few hours by my count," she says. She says this without looking away from the mirror. Herself looking at herself looking at herself looking at herself. This infinite loop of drunkenness and sadness in a perpetual loop.

"I doubt you would believe it if I told you," I say.

"Try me," she says.

"I've done some wrongs that I'd rather not do over again." I take another sip. "Might be the alcohol talking here, but I think I might have been wrong all my life."

The tip of an incisor pokes through my friend's smile in the mirror. "The next round is on me," she says. She slaps folded bills onto the counter. The bartender smiles and nods. He and I both assume that it's American money. We both assume that it's enough for us and our mirror twins.

"Thanks," I say.

"Talk. I could use a good story."

"You ever hear of Mad Maddy?" I ask.

15

EMMA

This man's vibe messes with the vibe of the place. I like the dark. The animal heads. The dark, dark wood. Reminds me of my father's place, his cabin, out in the woods when we'd go hunting. He taught me to shoot, to load, to kill.

Everything except field dress the damn deer.

I didn't have the stomach for that.

I do now.

This man—boy, really—goes on and on about how there's this rumor about a girl. She apparently haunts people through the mirror.

Except the way he tells the story, you can see that he's scared as he's telling it. A part of him wants to look into the mirror behind the bartender as he says all of this. His eyes get twitchy, like my daughter's hamster when we'd drop in a thick slice of apple for him to chew on.

And this man's light brown eyes dart back and forth between the mirror and me.

The funny thing is, as he talks just after looking into the mirror, his breathing and his speaking slow down some. Not a whole helluva lot, but enough for me to notice that it's taking him some time to get the words out and focus.

"Yes, yes," I say. "I know Mad Maddy." I take a sip of the freshly-poured whiskey. My man-boy buddy follows my lead.

His eyes widen. For a second he checks the mirror again and then rests his head on his hand, elbow propped up on the bar. He's trying not to look into the mirror again. He wants his focus to be on me, but he can't focus.

"You could say that I had a little bit of a problem with her when I was younger," I say.

Do I really want to do this? I ask myself. Is this something I want to do?

The boy takes out a pad of paper from his notebook and scribbles something down. It's a small spiral bound notebook, tiny pages that fit inside a coat pocket. Now I know what he reminds me of. That boy reporter from Superman. Jimmy Olsen.

I smirk and he looks at me, asking, "What's so funny?"

"You remind me of someone," I say. Take a sip. "That's all."

"Do you mind if I write this down?" he asks.

He already seems to be ready for my story. More than I am, truth be told. But I nod and point at his pen. "Sure, why not? So this Mad Maddy you're going on about?" I say. "She was friends with my daughter way back when."

"You don't say," he says. The boy scribbles something else on his pad of paper.

I go ahead and wait for him to finish. It'd be rude to continue without the audience's full participation, you see.

So I tell him:

So when I was such a young, young mother, my daughter and

Maddy used to play all the time. They were about seven years old. Maybe eight at this time.

She'd come over to the house and the girls would scream and chase each other and hide and play with their dolls all kinds outside. We had this beautiful lawn that was green all year. No brown or yellow spots. Even the damn dogs knew better than to ruin our lawn. My husband would likely go ballistic if they did anything to mess up that emerald beauty.

That's what he used to call the lawn. Yes, it had a nickname. My husband loved his lawn, what can I say? It's a southern thing.

One particular Saturday, we had some of my daughter's friends over. They ran around like usual. The dog chased them around, barking and barking.

I had just had my second child by then, so I was busy carrying poor Charles all over the house to get him to quiet down for his nap. It's not easy when you have three barking and screaming little creatures in the back house.

I opened the patio door. "Honey," I said, "you and your friend there, can you keep it quiet? I'm trying to put Charles to nap."

The girls nodded. "Yes, ma'am," they said in unison.

You know, you can say what you want about Madison scaring people, but she was a polite little girl. Nice. Clean. Always polite, the way a Southern gal ought to be.

Now Charles is one of those kids that never liked sleeping in his crib, so I left him in the swing. He liked that thing. Always seemed to calm him down. So, I wound it up and let it work its magic while I went to get snacks for the girls.

"Casey, honey," I yelled out to my daughter. "Could you please keep an eye on Charlie for me?"

Again, she nodded and it was interesting how quiet they all got all of a sudden. It is true what they say, you know, about how when kids get quiet, they're up to no good.

So I put my knife down and went back outside to check on the gals.

"Honey," I yelled. "What the hell are you doing?"

On Casey's little plastic table was Charlie, seated and dressed like a little doll at her tea table.

"We're having tea, mommy."

I smiled. It was cute, after all. "No dear, Charlie's too young for tea. Let him nap in his swing, please."

That's when Casey and Maddy both pouted. They pursed their lips and crosses their arms. I thought they were both going to throw a hissy fit. Turned out, Maddy came to her senses much faster than my own daughter.

"That's okay, ma'am," Maddy says to me. "We'll put him back in the swing."

"That would be great. Thank you, dear," I say to them.

And again, it gets quiet, but I watch them this time. From the kitchen counter, knife in hand and cutting crusts off the peanut butter and jelly sandwiches for the girls outside.

And that's when I get the plate and rest the pieces of sandwich on them. The girls hated the crusts, so I did what mommies do best and cut them off.

Except, my girl Casey, she always loved the crust. Hell, she was one of those weird kids that ate my crust and her broccoli and asparagus and Brussel sprouts. She ate anything and everything.

But when that girl Maddy came around, my Casey didn't like anything. Like a whole different child.

As I was saying, though, I step around to get a big plate for the sandwiches and when I turn around and go to the patio door, there is

Charlie again, sitting on the plastic table.

"I told you, let Charlie be. He needs to sleep."

"He was sleeping, mommy," says Casey. Except as she says this, she seems confused. She rests her hands on her hips and looks at Maddy. She wants to smile, but she bites her lips to keep her secret from me.

"What happened, then?" I ask. I rest the plate on the table and pick up my baby boy from his plastic seat. He doesn't say a single thing, still in that baby doll hat and his eyes wide open, staring at anything and everything.

"He just came over here," says Maddy.

That freaky, weird little girl.

"I'm sure he did," I say. "You're telling me I just missed my baby's first few steps? And that he came all the way over here to sit on this plastic table and have tea with you?"

I smile, nod, and put my boy back in the swing.

"Now you two eat up."

Charlie stays in the swing for maybe ten seconds before I pick him up again.

Fool me once, shame on you. Fool me twice, shame on me, right?

I figure then it's better to keep the baby in my reach. Just in case either my daughter or that creepy little girl was somehow lying to me. I wouldn't put it past either one of them, to be honest.

But when I'm back in the kitchen, cleaning up and whatnot, Charlie starts slapping my back. He's cooing like babies do.

His eyes are transfixed on something behind me.

So I turn around and ask Charlie what's the problem. Why he's all excited.

And my god damned grass was on fire.

The little creepy girl sat along the side of the porch, her legs tucked under her dress and her face staring directly into the fire.

And the girl, I swear she didn't do anything but stare and keep silent.

I ran to the back door as quickly as I could, still keeping Charlie balanced on my hip. The back door was locked, though. I don't know how that bitch did it, but she did it. Locked the back door from the outside.

"Where is she?" I scream at Maddy. "Where is my daughter?"

Maddy doesn't say anything, but taps against the closed glass of the door and then points at the yard.

My eyes follow her pointer finger and in the middle of the grass, in the deepest part of the yard, is my daughter rolling around in flames.

16

EMMA

It took me twenty minutes for the fire department to show up. I felt helpless just standing there. Watching her. The fire had begun to take up most of the sky.

The worst part?

I had to watch the whole damn thing from the inside. I had Charlie to look after. I couldn't let him just wander outside and watch his sister burn.

And Maddy...that bitch just stood there watching from the patio. I can't prove it. But I can swear, really swear, that she was smiling as she watched.

And I think, she did that on purpose. She knew what she was doing.

But that's crazy, right? That a five-year-old, a girl only five, would do this?

It took eighteen minutes, eighteen long, long minutes, for the firemen to arrive. Two minutes later, they were clearing out my house. The fire had reached the kitchen and dining area of my house. I had watched pictures that she had drawn, that my daughter had drawn for me. Everything burns up.

Sorry.

I don't normally open up this much.

But that girl. I don't think you know what you're doing. I don't think you know what you're opening up.

Because when I think about her, when I think about Maddy, all I see are my daughter's eyes.

I see the disappointment. I was supposed to protect her. I was supposed to see that she was in trouble.

But I couldn't. There was no way.

No one could see what kind of girl she was.

As the firemen took a set of our house I fought them as hard as I could. I didn't want to be away from my daughter. I couldn't be away from my daughter.

And Maddy just stood by.

I wish I had gone to her. I wish I could have asked her why?

But one of the firefighters, he had taken her back to her own house. After I had seen my daughter taken into the ambulance, after the surgeons told me what they could do for her, after I had seen my beautiful daughter's face scarred, I went to go see her.

Maddy, I mean.

I went to ask her why. I went to talk to her mother.

And yet?

And yet no one would answer. I stood at the door. I stood at that dark brown, wooden door. I slammed my fists into it. My knuckles were scraped up. When I got too tired, I slammed my head, my shoulders, into that door.

No one answered.

I guess I can't blame them. What you say, exactly? What do you say when your daughter set fire to someone else's house?

What do you say, when you know your daughter is a devil?

I even went to the police.

Want to know what they said? I remember marching into the station. The guy at the front desk stared at me like I was crazy. I guess I looked crazy. I had been crying all night. It's hard not to, you know?

So I tell this guy, Officer Dingus, that I want to press charges.

And he pulls out paper and asks me what happened. And I tell him about Maddy. I tell him about the fires and about her almost killing my daughter.

And the man quietly slips the paper back into its tray. His eyes never leave mine, and he says, "I'm sorry ma'am, there's nothing we can do."

Can you fucking believe that?

I remember resting my elbows on the counter. I remember looking into this man's eyes. And he stared back at me, and there was fear in his eyes. I think you recognize the name Maddy. That little girl, she was five years old, and grown men were afraid of her.

Or maybe it was the family.

Maybe everyone already knew something crazy about her, crazy about that family.

The man clasped both of his hands together. I think he was trying to hide the shaking.

My own fingers trembled from rage. His from fear.

At that point, I demanded to see the captain, a sergeant, anyone who would help me.

And the man was crafty. He stood up, looked me right in my eyes, and told me he would go get help. "But," he said, "I'm not sure who's available."

I waited there patiently for over two hours.

Then I went home.

My husband, Frank, barely talks to me. We slept in different rooms. I swore to him that I would do what I could to help Casey.

The silence in that house was louder than any of Charlie's screams. And that boy had a pair of lungs, let me tell you.

It was deafening.

So I went to the hospital. I left my son with my husband, talked to Frank through the closed bedroom door, and went to go see my baby Casey.

I stayed that night in the fire victims unit. The burn unit, I guess they call it. I read to my baby girl. I spoke to her, touched her through the bandages on every part Of her body.

For hours on end, she would just stare up at the white ceiling. I wanted to believe that she was just finding animals in the shadows. Watching the shapes of the popcorn ceiling and maybe connecting dots.

But I know what she was really doing. She was hating me. Maybe even hating herself.

I never did find out.

When they released her from the hospital, she had to come back months later for skin grafts. But it didn't matter. Her face wouldn't change. Nothing did. She looked like a half-melted Barbie doll. But her eyes used to be bright and blue and shiny with life and fun.

After that, she was gray. Sad. Depressed.

She barely left the house.

She went to school for about a year after that accident. Then, she wanted to be homeschooled.

We went through different wigs. Bandages. Glasses. Everything we could think of to keep her looking somewhat normal.

Jesus, I hate thinking that, you know? That she was ever not normal. Especially after that accident.

When Charlie got to be old enough to go into high school, Maddy had popped up again.

17

EMMA

Charlie was fourteen. He had grown up to be the typical awkward teenager. But such a handsome boy. Just like his father. He had a full head of blond hair. Long, because that was the style back then. And it looked good on him too. But those big green eyes, he got those from me.

He was tall, skinny. Could've played basketball if you wanted to. But that just wasn't his thing. He was into music. Which was fine, I guess. It was his way of dealing with his sister. You know, things like that, there just too difficult for a little kid to comprehend.

He was nine. When Casey — when she chose to leave us.

And so music was his thing.

And that, I guess, was how he met Maddy.

They were in the same music class. Somehow Maddy had moved away, and then moved back here. I don't know where she went. She never really talked to me after that.

But she talked to Charlie every day. And Charlie had somehow bought it all.

At first, Charlie tried to hide it from me. He tried to hide that they were hanging out.

Charlie was fourteen. He wanted the girls to like him. And Maddy had shown, and extreme I guess, interest in Charlie.

At least that's what I imagined.

Back then Charlie had gotten his first cell phone. I was hesitant to buy it. It meant a whole new kind of freedom that I wasn't ready to give a little fourteen-year-old boy.

But I guess I felt guilty, you know?

Charlie was an only child now. I wanted to give them everything. I couldn't be the father that didn't walk out on him. I couldn't give him the sister. We were all we had. And I wanted them happy.

So when he said he wanted a cell phone, I got him a cell phone.

Every evening that tall, lanky boy would disappear up into his room. He said he was doing homework.

Sometimes I believed him.

Other times he said he was talking to someone. Maybe he was talking to his friends. I barely saw him hang out with anyone. And maybe he was just on his computer. Doing, you know, what teenage boys do.

I guess it had been a couple of months when I finally decided to check. He was sleeping that night. It was a school night so he was in bed early.

And when I checked his phone, checking his messages, I saw this number that he had talked to. A lot.

The next day, I asked Charlie about it.

"Mom, why are you asking me this?" he said.

"Because," I told him. "A mother is supposed to."

He stared at me over his breakfast cereal. I swear he must've blinked only twice in the last ten minutes. Shoveling the Cheerios into his mouth, chewing slowly. He was judging me.

He knew it wasn't cool to talk to his mom.

He might've been weighing his options. Or maybe he was lying to me the whole time.

I know you were once a teenage boy, sir. But you little teenage boys are hell on a mama's soul. I know teen girls get a bad rap. We all know they get their mood swings. Sometimes it's hormones, sometimes it's that time of the month.

But what your mama probably spared you, sir, was the fact that you, too, was also an emotional wreck. I see you smilin', because it's the truth.

You know it, too.

And just so you know, I'm proud to say this. I did let them off the hook. Instead, I took a different route.

I took away his driving privileges, and I drove him to his next date.

At least that's what I told him was going to happen.

At that point, I got whatever I wanted from Charlie.

He began to tell this elaborate story of him and Maddy going to the prom together. It was then, that I felt this deep fire in my gut.

"Charlie, you can't go to the prom with that girl. You know what she did to your sister."

"Mom, I can make my own decisions."

"No, you can't. I am making this decision for you." I grabbed my dinner plate from the table and brought it into the kitchen. He followed me thereafter.

"I don't see why this is such a big deal, Mom. It was an accident. She told me."

"Oh, is that what you told you? You are one-year-old. You have no idea what I saw. I was there. I know what happened. I saw what happened to your sister. You have no right to believe her."

He stared at me. I can see him biting his lower lip. Charlie always did that, when he was upset. I had always worried about crooked teeth. Maybe even him chewing through his lip someday. But he was never an angry kid.

At least not until that day.

That day he stared at me like he had fire in his eyes. Like, like the fire that I saw that day. And you have to believe me, that wasn't my normal Charlie. That boy staring back at me, that wasn't my boy.

"Charlie," I told him, "you're not going with that girl. There's no way I will let you leave this house to see her."

Charlie took that plate, with half his dinner still left on it, and he placed it on the counter. Then he stormed upstairs.

There was no talking to that boy. Not when he's like that.

That night, I sat on the couch and stared at the television. I don't even know what I was watching. I dismember flashing lights, people laughing, doors being opened and closed, situations that were supposed to be funny. But all I could think about was how much I angered Charlie. And I thought, maybe I was wrong. Maybe it was an accident.

But that felt wrong to my gut. I mean, I lost my daughter. She had taken her own life. Because of her. But maybe it shouldn't have been such a big fight.

So I go upstairs, to Charlie's room. And for a second, I think maybe I can hear him talking to Maddy. Maybe I can prove that she was behind everything.

David Gearing

But as I held me are close, I didn't hear anything. No TV. No radio. No typing, no clicking. So I open the door.

And instead of where I think my boy should be, there's nothing. An empty bed.

And an open window.

18

EMMA

When I got downstairs and open the door, there wasn't a sign of anything. No cars. No one waiting outside. Wherever Charlie was, he was out there.

With her.

I do know where to go. And of course, the worst went through my mind. I could just imagine that girl, Maddy, setting Charlie on fire. Pulling a gun on him. Doing, I don't know, something terrible.

So naturally, I try the police. And they were useless.

They say to me, there's no way they can file a missing persons report. He's just a stupid teenager, no need to be worried.

"But no," I tell him, "he's out there. With Maddy. We both know that means trouble."

There is silence on the other end. I can hear his breathing. Maybe he was thinking. Maybe he was holding back laughter.

But when I said Maddy, I could feel the whole shift in mood.

"Ma'am," he says to me. "There's nothing we can do."

I had heard that before.

Maybe it's true. There was nothing they could do. But I could do plenty.

So I drove in my minivan to where I thought Maddy must've lived. I don't remember her moving. And I'm still convinced she didn't. But, when I got there, no one claimed to know who she was.

Sure as shit, they were complete strangers living there. The man who answered the door, he was white, but, not white. Maybe European. Maddy's family, I don't know where they were from, but it wasn't Europe.

And I was tempted to give up. There wasn't much else I could do, except maybe wait.

So I parked the minivan in a garage, and waited.

I fell sleep in that van. The power of exhaustion, anxiety at its finest. I'm honestly surprised I was able to sleep.

So of course, I don't know how long I was in that van before Charlie came walking down the street. He was wearing the same clothes, white T-shirt, blue jeans his favorite blue skater shoes. But in his hands, he was holding a plastic bag, a brown plastic bag. It hung low, rounded on the bottom. It looked heavy in his hand. And he carried it like it was precious. He was careful not to swing around. Whatever was in it, it was dark in color.

As Charlie got closer, I could see the expression on his face—it changed. He seemed to just stare, looking forward. I'm not sure he knew he was going home. Like autopilot, you know?

His legs just seemed to carry him home. He didn't have an honest expression on his face, until I got out of the van.

"Charlie," I said. "Where the hell were you?" From here I could tell his hands were dark red. Like dipped in paint, or blood.

Charlie's face seemed to break from the emotionless mask I had seen walking down the street. He looked at me like it was the first time you see me in months. When he blinked, tears welled up in his eyes.

I took a step forward to hug him, but he took a step back.

"Charlie," I said, "what's going on? What happened? Where were you?"

Charlie shook his head. "I don't know." He took another step back.

"When you mean? You don't know? How do you walk down the middle of the night, and not know where you're coming from?"

Charlie just stared at me. He stared at me, stared through me, and blinked. He shook his head again. "I don't know."

I pointed at the bag that dangled from his right hand. "What's that?"

Charlie held it up for me to look at it. Almost offering it to me.

I grab the bag by the handles, and tried to look inside. But that smell, let me tell you.

It was something heavy, something that used to be a life. I dropped the bag.

"What the hell is that? What did you bring home? Did Maddy give that to you?"

Charlie shook his head again. "I don't know."

Charlie began to bite his lip.

I helped Charlie get back inside the house, then went back outside to check what was inside the bag. Search for a stick, and pried the bag open.

Wanna know what I saw?

A god damn heart. I don't know what kind of heart. Too small for a cow. Maybe too big for a dog, or a cat.

I don't want to say what I thought it was, or where I thought it came from. I can't think of my Charlie that way.

But this was Maddy, you know? That little witch was capable of anything.

I didn't tell anyone about that bag, you know. I couldn't. How do you explain that?

Do you know anyone missing heart? My son brought one back.

My family was already broken enough. I didn't need this, too.

So I took the bag, and tossed it in the trash outside.

19

JAMES

Emma finished her drink and tossed more money onto the counter. As she looked at me, I could see her measuring the disbelief in my eyes.

"You don't believe me," she said.

I shook my head. "No."

My finger began tracing imaginary numbers along the top of the counter. My grandfather. Charlie. Something didn't quite add up here. I looked up at Emma.

"The math just doesn't add up. There's no way your Charlie could have known Maddy. Not unless he was eighty-five years old. In looking at you, Charlie is what? Thirty-five? Forty?"

Emma stands up, slides off her seat, and rests one hand on my shoulder. Her pale, green eyes stare at me. She makes sure she has my attention. Her lips tense. Her job tenses. Then she rolls her eyes and smiles. "Fine," she says, "want me to take you to him?"

I smile. "Interesting proposition."

"I can tell you don't believe me. Last thing I want you to think is I'm a liar."

When she takes her hand off my shoulder, she reaches for her clutch purse on the seat and holds it closely to her chest.

But her eyes stay locked with mine.

I wave at the bartender, and he comes my way resting his hands on the counter. "What can I get ya?"

"One more shot." Something tells me I'm going to need it. I toss ten dollars onto the counter, down the shot of whiskey, and follow Emma out the door.

Fifteen minutes later and were strolling upon a small apartment complex just south of the city. It's maybe three buildings, two stories. Only four families per building. Charlie's is the second building.

Emma stands in front of the door, I stand behind Emma. The doors are all a dark red, something like maroon. And metal. Not wood.

And I notice that even Emma looks unsure as she stands in front of the door. She holds her hand up, makes a fist, but freezes.

"Something wrong?"

She shakes her head. "No, it's just been a long time."

"Listen, we don't have to do this."

Emma brings herself to knock on the door. "No, I need to do this."

We stand there for about five seconds, and no one comes to answer the door. Emma knocks again.

There's some shuffling behind the door, and then finally the doorknob turns. The child's head appears in the narrow space between the door and the door frame. His eyes are wide, bright green. He looks at me, and his eyes narrow. But when he sees Emma, he swings the door wide open and grabs her leg hugging it tightly.

"Grammy!"

The kid has to be something like five years old. His hair is dark, stringy, and cut into a bowl cut. He's wearing a Spiderman shirt that barely masks the SpaghettiOs stain on his shoulder. And somehow this morning, he forgot to wear pants.

Emma pats the boy on the head, and leans down to kiss his forehead. "Is your father home?"

The boy shakes his head no, and grabs Emma's hands and leads her into the living room.

"What do you mean no? Are you home alone?"

"He went to the store," the boy said. He looks at me, and his eyes narrow again. He doesn't trust me." I'm what he would call stranger danger. It's a good instinct to have.

Even for a five-year-old boy.

I hold my breath and take a step inside the apartment, closing the door behind me.

I'm surrounded by pictures, reflective surfaces. The pictures are professionally framed baby photos. The reporter part of me can't take my eyes off the pictures, but my fear makes my heart stand still as I take a look.

I try not to stand still for too long. If I stay in front of one of the surfaces, and she can come get me. The only safe room, it seems, is the kitchen. So I walk in there and examine the pile of dishes in the sink. Two days' worth. Maybe. Inside the kitchen, wooden cabinets. White magnetic refrigerator. No reflective surfaces. For now, I'm safe.

But Emma comes into the kitchen, and she opens the refrigerator. Pitcher, and pours herself a glass of water from a mug in the sink. She takes a drink, then looks at me. "Are you thirsty?"

"No. I don't think I can drink right now."

Emma nods knowingly. She pours herself another drink, sits down, and puts the mug back in the sink. "Where did you say your father went?"

The boy sits back in his father's recliner, his feet barely touch the ground. He looks comfortable, but his eyes keep watch at the door. Like he's not supposed to be there. The recliner is old, with a patch just below the armrest. Some burn holes along the left armrest. Some dark stains..

It gives his chair character, my Pop Pop would say.

Emma once again stands in front of me, by the entryway to the living room. She folds her arms across her chest and watches her grandson. She looks like she's about to say something when the door opens.

Squeaky footsteps and a crinkling paper bag. The footsteps are slow, unassuming.

The owner of the feet that made those footsteps rests the bag on the kitchen counter, and he seems not surprised by me. "And you are?"

I smile not out of being friendly, but out of instinct. It's my default when I am afraid. Either that, or I laugh.

I open my mouth but nothing comes up.

That's when Emma saves the day. "Is that how you greet your mother?"

Charlie, I presume, opens his arms wide, and hugs his mother. But there's something cold behind it. It's a quick hug, not the type of hug for people who haven't seen each other in a long, long time. They break away, and it's as if they haven't known each other for years.

"Funny, you don't look eighty-five years old."

Charlie shoots Emma a glance, his eyes widening. "Mom?"

Emma smiles while shaking her head. "He doesn't believe that you met her."

"Her?" Charlie begins putting away some of his groceries from the paper bag. Box of dried spaghetti, milk, jar of tomatoes.

"You know, Charlie. You know which her I'm talking about."

Charlie shakes his head. "No, mom. I told you to stop this." He looks at me and smiles, folds the paper bag, and tucks it under his arm. "I'm sorry, sir, but my mom is a little crazy."

"Thank you," I say. "Honestly, I sort of figured as much." Turning to Emma, I say, "I guess I'll head back into town."

Emma stops me, holding onto my elbow. "No, I promised you. Charlie has the answers you want."

A loud puff of frustration of Charlie as he sighs, rubs his hands through his hair.

"Fine," he says. Charlie motions at a chair at his kitchen table. "Please, sir. Have a seat."

I do as he says, and Emma smiles. Charlie looks like he wants to throw up.

"If you're here about Maddy, then I guess I have to tell you something first." He steps out into the hallway and shouts up the stairs. "Philip! Get down here, please."

The little boy stumbles down the steps and enters into the kitchen. The boy says nothing, but he raises an eyebrow and looks at each of the adults in the room.

Charlie motions him to come over. The boy does. Charlie rests his hands on Philip's shoulders. "Sir," Charlie says.

"Please," I say, "call me James."

"Well then, Philip, meet Mr. James. Mr. James, meet Philip, Maddy's son."

20

JAMES

"Is this a game?" I take a better look at the boy, and I can't exactly deny that he might be telling the truth. He has Charlie's wide mouth, but the look in Phillip's eyes...that's all Maddy. "This isn't a fucking joke."

Philip seems to pull back, retreating deeper into his father's embrace.

In those eyes. Those eyes have haunted me for the last twenty years. Since I can remember.

Charlie pats Philip on the head. "Why don't you go play in the other room?" The adults wait for the child to disappear before Charlie looks at me raising his eyebrows. "Listen, you don't have to believe me. But let's keep from the bad language and from disparaging his mother in front of the boy, can we?"

"So then where is his mother?" I ask.

Charlie pulls out a chair. He sits down at the end of the table. The mood in the room gets serious. At first, I thought Charlie was a fraud. Maybe he still is. This is also painful for him.

And this whole thing seems far-fetched. Maddy, having a kid? Being able to have a kid?

But those eyes...

Those eyes were the reason I was on sleeping pills since I was seven. Why I avoided mirrors for the last twenty-five years. Why I couldn't drive.

"Those eyes haunted me when I was a child. I saw them in pools of water. In the water I would drink. In the mirror."

Charlie nods, knowingly. "They were beautiful, weren't they?"

This Charlie is a sick bastard.

"Yeah, well, can I use the bathroom?"

Charlie stands up, "Here," he says, "Let me show you where."

"No," I hold my hands up. "I can find it. No need to show me."

Charlie sits back down and crosses his legs. "It's upstairs."

I nod.

The entire hallway is white, and mostly bare. Not many pictures anywhere. Nothing for me to see what Maddy looks like. And yet, as I find the stairs, and I take gradual steps, I feel like she's right here.

There are times when I catch myself holding my breath. And looking out, upstairs, I feel like if I breathe then this is all real.

Fortunately, it's a short trip to the bathroom. The doors wide open. Ceramic tiles on the floor. I wouldn't medicine cabinet.

And of course, a giant mirror on the wall above the sink.

I had prepared for this.

At least I thought I did.

I turn away from the mirror. Keep my eyes on the door as I walk into the bathroom. I close the door behind me. It's dark, and I can't tell if I want to open a window. Or turn on the lights.

For safety's sake, and so I don't pee all over the floor, I figure the lights will have to do.

I can't not look. Into the mirror. My heart stops at every blink. Every time, I expect her to be there. Staring at me. Dark gray eyes. A smile, dark and twisted. Dark red lips.

The nightmare.

Through quick, sneaky glances I kept my eyes on her world.

It was half fear, half perversion, that kept me staring into the mirror.

And sometimes, I think I saw a finger. Not my finger. Hers.

Sometimes I think I see an eyeball.

And as much as I try, I just can't go.

I try standing. I try sitting. And nothing.

Figure maybe, maybe this whole situation just has me too freaked out.

And so, I try to leave.

My trick is, I keep my eyes closed when I open the door. I have this down to a science now. I know how far have to stand away. I know how far the door is open. I know when it's safe to leave.

It's not that difficult. Blind people do it all the time.

And I do this, without even taking a glance at the mirror.

But as I leave the bathroom, Philip comes down the hallway. His bedroom must be at the end of the hallway. There's a poster, a Spiderman poster on the door.

Philip waves at me, but he doesn't smile. His eyes stay locked on mine.

He pauses about two feet away from me. He wants to talk, I can see it in his lips. But something keeps him from talking to me.

His light brown hair dangles from his face. He finally opens his mouth. "Are you done?"

I nod and nudge the door open. "She's all yours." He nods at me, manages a smile, and walks into the bathroom. The door shuts with a loud click.

My hands grab the wooden bar that serves as the railing for the stairs and there's a creepy sense of silence.

This feels weird, but I go back upstairs, and say, "Are you okay?"

My question is met with silence.

"Are you okay, do you need any help?"

Silence.

I wait for a second, count to three, and decide maybe he's just shy. I used to be the same way when I was his age.

When I turn my back, something hits the floor. The sound echoes like plastic. A plastic cup, the kind you use for toothbrushes.

Then, heavier thump on the floor.

I tap on the door. "Hey, Philip, are you okay?" More silence.

I catch myself holding my breath again. My hand shakes. So I grasp the door handle with both hands, hoping one of them can keep the other still. It doesn't work.

One.

Two.

Three.

With my eyes closed, I open the door. The lights are off. I can't bring myself to look into the mirror, but I know she's there. Watching me. Watching him.

Maybe it's my imagination, but I can feel her fingers, like claws, along the nape of my neck. Her heavy breathing along my cheek.

I pry my eyes open just a little, and there's Philip huddled in the corner.

"Come on," I say. I hold my hand out, but he refuses to touch it. Even shakes his head violently.

"No," he whispers.

"You have to leave," I say.

He shakes his head again. Whispers, "No."

And we both know we don't have time for this.

I reach out, grab his wrists, and barrel through the bathroom door. It's only two quick steps to the stairs, no time to stop. My arms wrap around Philip. I try to keep him close as we tumble down the stairs.

My body feels like it hits every stair, slams into every wall. My shoulders feel bruised, ribs broken. Philip tries to wriggle from my grasp. I look up, and to my surprise no one is there. Everyone must be outside.

Philip tries again, wrestling from my grip. He kicks in my knees. Even try screaming, but I hold my hand over his mouth.

She's out to get us. She's out to get him.

We have to be safe. I can't let him fall prey, too.

"We have to go."

Philip kicks in my knees.

But my grip stays steady. He's in my grasp, I can't let him go. We have to be safe.

I have to protect him.

For a little kid, he doesn't weigh a lot. So it's easy to pick him up charge down the stairs and look for the front door. When I stop, looking down the hallway, there's the only picture I can see. It's a framed picture of Santa Claus and a green box, gift wrapped for somebody. A tag on the box says "daddy."

It's a picture, from Philip.

But the face I see in the glass, it's not mine. It's hers. She smiles with her red, dark lips. Her face pale.

I hold my breath again. Just pick a direction. Any direction.

In charge down that direction. It takes me half a second to realize the front doors in front of us.

But then, so is Emma.

"What are you doing?" she says.

"No time, we have to go." With Philip tucked underneath my arm, I reach for the front door and snap it open. I'm out the door before I can exhale. Pass the driveway when I inhale. Halfway down the block when I exhale again. I don't know how long it is before I hear the engine behind me. Philip seems dumbfounded.

His eyes are wide open. His mouth gaping open.

I think he's in shock. Maybe he thinks this is fun.

But the sound of the engine doesn't disappear. I turn around, looking over my shoulder.

And it's Emma. She motions for me to go to the sidewalk. She rolls down the window, pulls up next to me. "Get in," she says. "I'll drive."

21

JAMES

We have been driving down side roads I've never seen before for almost fifteen minutes when she finally uses the word kidnap.

"What has gotten into you?"

I have to have all the windows rolled down. My view stays on the house is passing by us. I shake my head. "She was there."

Emma shakes her head. "We mean by that? Who was where?"

The car slows down. She flicks on the blinker, and turns right.

"Emma, Maddy. Maddy was there. She was after him."

"Philip?" Emma tries to shoot a smile at her grandson in the back seat. "Maddy was after Philip?"

"Or me. Or me through him. I don't know. But she was there." I take a look at Emma and I can see the frustration on her face. But it's not a scared frustration. She's entertained, maybe even expected this.

"You don't believe me," I say.

"Yes. I do. I think."

Philip lays down in the back seat, tucks his arms behind his head, and closes his eyes.

The barbecue smell of burnt wood wafts into the car, giving my stomach permission to grumble. It had been I don't know how many hours since I had eaten something.

"Maybe we should feed the boy," I mutter.

Emma looks into the backseat and smiles. "He'll be fine. He's napping right now."

"Why is he not freaking out?" I ask.

"Because he loves his grandmother," Emma says with a smile. Her wrinkles grow deeper around her eyes and the corners of her mouth as she smiles. She believes it, at least. That much I can tell. "So where do we go?" she asks.

A rebel without a plan. This sums up my life perfectly.

I can only rub my hands through my hair and then bury my face in my elbows. "I don't know." I want to scream. The air gathers in my chest. There's a slight roar in my throat as I speak. "I don't know. I don't know. I don't know."

"Then why did you kidnap my grandson?"

"Because he was unsafe."

Emma thinks she's slick. She turns the car into a motel and flicks off the parking lights. We park in a spot furthest away from the front door and she turns to me. "We can't really hide out for the rest of your life. My son probably already has the police looking for us."

"But you're his grandmother."

"Do you know how much power that's going to hold up in court, James?" Emma lets herself relax into the seat. She stares at the ceiling of the cab like it's the night sky. "Why did I let you do this?"

"Why did you introduce me?"

"Because I thought maybe you could get the answers you wanted."

We sit in the car, silent. We marinate in the potential answers either one of us could give to that rhetorical question.

But it's pointless, really.

"Maybe we return the kid."

"Phillip?" Emma says. "The kid has a name."

"I'm sorry. Philip."

Emma smiles, nods. "If you really want to know," she says. "I introduced you because I needed to know if Maddy was still alive."

"I had only assumed she was dead," I say. "I can't think of anyone who haunts from the living."

Emma grips the car's steering wheel with both hands and squeezes so tight her knuckles who white. "I want her to be alive. She's taken so much from me."

A phone starts to ring.

Emma looks at me. I return the glance. "It's not me," I say.

Emma fidgets for her phone and pulls out a little pink cell phone. She answers it after squinting at the number. "Hello," she says.

The voice on the other end is male. A deep voice. Charlie's.

"No, this isn't a joke," Emma says. "Yes, we'll return him."

There's a mess of noises from the other side. Emma pulls the phone away from her ear and she covers the mouthpiece. She whispers, "I'm sorry."

When the voice stops screaming, there's a moment of silence until Emma fills the void.

"He's right here," she says. She peers into the backseat. "Yes, he's fine. He's perfectly fine. Maybe a bit startled."

I slap my forehead. Hinting at pain and frustration in a child is not a good calming tactic. Especially when you're being accused of kidnapping.

"We'll bring him home tomorrow," she finally says. The voice on the other end grows silent. "Let him spend some time with his grandmother, and then we'll return him home to you."

She barely leaves him time to say goodbye and then hangs up the phone. She lets the phone drop out of her hands and onto the floor by her feet.

"I'm sorry," I say.

She waves it off with her hand. "Don't be," she says. "We need to find Maddy."

"What does that mean?" I ask.

"I want answers," she says. "For taking my daughter from me."

"But if she's dead, you won't be finding any answers."

Emma exits the car, opens the backseat. "Come here, honey," she says.

Philip barely wakes up. He stares at me as Emma picks him up and holds him close to her chest.

Then Emma begins her walk toward the front door of the building.

"We're sleeping here?" I ask.

Emma keeps walking. She pats Philip's head and whispers into his ear. "Would that be fun?" she says. "Like five-star camping."

"But we can't stay here," I say. "I don't have any money."

"We have enough money," Emma shouts out to me. "Trust me."

I follow her, putting a healthy distance between us. She walks fast, even with a boy in her arms. She walks with a dedication and a confidence that is rare in women half her age. I get the feeling as she's walking, however, that she's enjoying all of this.

I imagine she's missed having a grandson around. Maybe even missed having children around.

I get the feeling that what I did was a fortunate event for Emma. Now she gets a kid to take care of, a substitute for what she lost with Casey.

These thoughts corral themselves in my head until I'm nearly five feet from turning the corner and facing the front glass doors.

The night sky was beginning to sparkle with stars. Out here, there are few lights with the exception of the heavy, bright sign along the front yard announcing to all drivers and passersby that this place had rooms to rent for the night.

And yet, glass doors. You couldn't avoid them in this day and age.

Emma stops just short of the door, her hand resting on the handle. "What's the matter with you?" she says. "Come on."

I stand still, holding my arms behind me and stare away. "I can't."

She winces, narrows her eyes. "Why? A phobia of motels?" She smiles, and I can see her trying to figure out a joke in there somewhere.

"No," I say. Shaking my head, I mutter, "Fear of mirrors."

Emma lets go of the door. "Let Grandma have her shoulders back, okay?" She sets Philip down and comes over toward me. "So it's true?" she says.

"What?" I mutter. "What's true?"

"It's true," she says again, slowly. "That she comes in through the mirrors."

"It's an old tale that everyone talks about. But yes," I say. "It's true. I know it sounds ridiculous as it comes out of my mouth. These things don't happen. But I damn near get a heart attack every time I have to walk into a bathroom. I couldn't drive until I had years of therapy."

Emma grabs hold of Philip's hand and offers to go get the room for us, leaving me outside.

I sit with my back against the wall and stare up into the sky. It's a light blue sky this time at night. Not quite dark enough to see every little planet, but it's beautiful nonetheless.

They say that when you look up into the sky, you're seeing the past. The light that left these stars left them years and years and years ago. The sunlight you get burned from? That left the sun nearly eight minutes before it lit up the daytime sky.

"What did you see, Maddy? What's the truth?"

Emma emerges from the office holding a key card in her hand. She nods toward the walkway, down to the steps, and up the hallway to our room.

I follow her, walking briskly and trying to not look into the windows. So many reflective surfaces.

So many lights and images.

Finally, the boy speaks. "What's wrong with him?" Philip says.

I bite my tongue, looking away.

"Nothing's wrong with him," Emma says. "He's just tired. That's all."

Philip keeps his hand in his grandmother's tight grip, but he looks at me, over his shoulder.

There's a thin, creepy grin. Then he turns to face his grandmother again. "Can we eat soon?" he says.

Emma finds the door and lets us in. The light flicks on.

At the end of the room, a six-foot wide mirror that reflects all of us back to ourselves. Mirror images of ourselves staring back at us.

"Please," I say and flick off the lights.

Philip goes for the bed furthest away from us, toward the bathroom.

The room smells like someone had been smoking in it. This despite the no smoking sign on the nightstand between the two twin-sized beds.

We have no clothing to luggage so Emma plops down next to her grandson and rubs his back. "What are you hungry for?" she asks.

Philip says the first place he sees when he looks out the mirror. "Burger King."

The restaurant's familiar logo beams at us like a lighthouse to harboring ships.

"And your father lets you eat that stuff?" she says.

Philip nods and smiles. "Yes."

"You're lying," Emma says. She taps him gently and playfully on his nose. "But I'm your grandma and I outrank your father." She grabs keys and flips them around in her fingers. "I won't tell if you don't."

Philip nods in agreement. He gathers himself up by the pillows, still covered with an orange and red cover. There's supposed to be a pattern of flowers on the covers, but I just can't see it.

I plant my ass on my side of the bed and watch Emma get to the front door. "Are you coming?"

Philip hops out of the bed and runs to Emma's side.

She looks at me. "And you?"

I shake my head, then nod. Finally letting my face fall into my hands. "Ugh. I don't know. Yes, I guess."

I stand up, follow them to the front door. I'm the last to leave, the last one closing the door on our way out.

And as I do so, a light comes on in the bathroom.

It's Maddy. In the mirror, but something looks different.

She smiles, her eyes looking darker than before. Heavy circles around her cheeks. "See you later," she says.

22

JAMES

"He's walking kinda fast," Philip says.

I'm across the parking lot, standing on the grassy edge of the sidewalk for almost thirty whole seconds before the other two finally catch up with me.

"Yes, he is, honey. But you keep with me, okay?"

Philip nods. He turns and smiles at me.

I try to smile back, but when I look at his face, I see hers.

I can't hide the shudder that travels from the base of my tailbone to my shoulders.

"Are you cold?" Emma says.

I shake my head. "No," I say. "Just a chill."

We cross the street. Emma holding onto Philip, practically dragging him across the street. Me following not too far behind.

The parking lot of the Burger King isn't as busy as it looks inside. A line has formed that goes from the counter to the doorway. There seems to be someone even standing in the foyer.

I pause.

Emma pauses and turns around. "More windows," she says.

I nod.

"Do you want to stay here?" she says. "I can get the food."

I hold my breath, count to three. My eyes go from the reflective windows to Emma's caring face. "No, I can try to brave it."

"That's a lot of reflective windows," she says. "Are you sure?"

I nod. "There's a lot of people around. I'll be safe."

Emma grasps Philip's hand walks into the building.

The door swings closed. I stand on the outside.

They open a second register and the line splits in half. Emma and Philip move to the back of the second line and wait patiently. She points to the menu just above their heads and Philip seems to be speaking something back.

I rest my hand on the mirrored glass.

From deep beneath the glass, something seems to touch my hand back.

Something warm.

I release everything, pull my hand from the door and run to the side of the building. There is some outside seating with a thick plastic orange and white umbrella to block out the sun.

"I can't do this," I mutter to myself.

The window is covered with paint to my right. It advertises something I don't care to read. All I know is, right now, I feel safe.

Safe as I panic into my arm and elbow.

Some people come out of the building and slow down as they walk past me.

They talk about me. I can hear every little syllable. Some sounds stronger than others. The hard pop of t's and d's. The soft yet judgmental sound of s's.

When I look up, everything turns around, stares at the empty space in front of them and speak to each other in hushed whispers.

"Get away from me," I blurt out.

The couple just coming out of the building is dressed warm. A white man, black woman. They hold hands, grabbing their bags with clenched fists. The woman turns to look at me. She wants to smile, but the man tells her to turn her head.

"Fuck you," I mutter.

The man almost stops, but the woman nudges him. "Leave him alone," she says. "He's probably homeless."

The two disappear into a car and drive off.

Looking into the reflective windows is not an option.

So I stand up, pacing the sitting area. I can get from one side to the next in seven steps. Eight if I don't try to stride too much.

But I make a mistake. I look up, glancing at a beaming light that seems to strobe in the distance. It's a motorcycle, the front light flickering to warn drivers that it's on the road.

But in the distance, in the three cars that sit parked next to each other, a hand pokes at the glass.

Even this far away—some ten, maybe twenty feet away—from the cars, I can hear the tapping.

Hard, pressing taps with a sharp, heavy fingernail against the thick, shatter-resistant glass.

"No," I mutter. "No. Not here. I'm safe outside."

The tapping gets louder. In all of the windows, all of the mirrors, hands.

Hands tapping. Some tapping in unison. Others tapping out at a random, torturous pattern.

My legs give out and I'm on the ground before I can turn to run away.

The door to the Burger King squeaks as it opens.

I try to scramble to my feet, but someone grabs my shoulder.

I don't know who. I can't see faces with my eyes closed.

My hands reach for the mystery person's hands, slamming him down into the ground. The body grunts and moans in pain.

It's a man. Not a boy.

I can't open my eyes. I don't want to see.

So I stand up, blind. I lodge my foot into the man's stomach, pressing hard. His skin feels tight like a fresh trampoline. But soon, it goes soft.

The guy screams, tries to push me off but fails. When he rolls to his side, I stumble for a moment but catch my balance.

And Maddy is right there, staring at me.

She waves, smiles. Her dark, stringy hair hangs in front of her eyes.

Then more tapping.

Tap. Tap. Tap.

My foot hits the bag the man dropped.

I launch it at one of the cars. The bag splats. Wet stains engulf the insides of the bag.

But the tapping continues.

Tap. Tap-tap. Tap.

Rocks. She can't stay there if the windows are broken.

I seize a rock from the ground, gripping it tightly in my knuckles.

My first slam into the window gives it a slight crack.

"She can't live here," I mutter.

I can hear voices back behind me.

Maybe hers.

Maybe someone else's.

It doesn't matter.

Shatter the glass. Break it all.

The first window—a rear passenger window to a light blue sedan of some kind—cracks, then breaks when I force my fist through it.

My fingers feel warm and sticky. When I peel the fingers apart, the blood stretches thin, then breaks into streams down my knuckles.

But the tapping hasn't stopped.

So I grab the rock again and slam it into the next car.

Windows refuse to break, but I'm shattering what I can. Busting my knuckles against the windows.

Finally, someone grabs my shoulders and yanks me backwards.

My feet give out beneath me. The dark sky blurs into the colors of cars and stars and clouds into a confusing swirl and shades.

A warm surge of pain bounces through my ass and my shoulders.

For a moment, I can only stare.

"Jesus fucking Christ, James," Emma says. "What's gotten into you?"

"He's bleeding," the kid says.

Emma pats him on the shoulder. "Leave the food here, honey. Go inside and get the manager. Get someone to call an ambulance."

"No," I say. I try to blink and manage one eye at a time. "No, no ambulance."

Emma stands up and waves her hands. "Philip!" she shouts. "No ambulance. Just go sit down, honey, okay?"

He disappears into the crowd and into the building.

"What happened?" Emma says. She offers a hand but pulls it away when she sees my own fists covered in my blood.

"She was here," I mutter. "I saw her. Laughing. Tapping."

"You broke that?" Emma says. She points at a car.

I stare. Processing the question.

I know what she's asking. But I don't know if I did it.

She pulls me up by grabbing my wrists. The only part of my arms that seems to be blood-free. When I'm standing, she pulls her purse back over her shoulder and just shakes her head. Her hands turn me away from the car and the damage I've caused.

"Come on," she says. "We need to go."

A person comes out of the building followed by Philip. "What the actual fuck, man?"

The man works here, wearing a dark brown shirt with a picture of a hamburger on it. In red letters, it reads Have it your way. His dark red hair is held back by a dark brown visor that shields his eyes from my view.

"Please," Emma says. She wraps her arm around my shoulders. "He needs help. Medication," she says.

I shake my head. But I see what she's doing.

"Just let us get his medication. He's not dangerous."

The man steps off the cement steps of the building and comes over to his car. "I don't care if he's dangerous," the man says. "I'm gonna be fucking dangerous if you don't pay for this."

Emma shakes her head. "I don't really have the money. It was an accident."

The man motions for someone to go inside. "Call the fucking police, then."

But before the man can lower his hand and adjust his cap, we all hear some jingling change and then a loud clicking sound.

We all look up and see that it's Emma's ring tapping against the handle of a .38 mm handgun.

23

JAMES

"Grammy?" Philip mutters then pushes through the crowd.

Emma nods slowly, but tries to keep the gun away from Philip's view. She maneuvers around the crowd. Her back shifts to block Philip's view of the weapon at every step. She stops when she is directly in between the asshole in the visor and Philip.

"Stay there, honey."

From where he's standing, I can see Philip just fine. He's smiling. With her eyes.

"Emma, put it away."

Emma nods.

The entire crowd takes a step back. The asshole rests his hands on his head and gets down on his knees.

He's been through this before, I see.

"What are you doing, man?" Asshole mutters. "I wasn't gonna do nothing. I just wanted my damned money."

"I said we don't have any money," Emma mutters. I can see her shoulders relax a little. She begins to grimace, her smile tight-lipped.

"It's fine, man. It's fine. Just fucking go already."

"You promise?' Emma says. "We can go?"

My hands feel like freezing fire. Each throb in my knuckles pushes more blood out of the gaping wound I have along the sides of my hand. The small shards of glass have either been pushed in or pulled out by my rubbing them together.

"Fire. Electric. Freezing. Fire. Everything pulsing in my hands.

"Can we go? Please?" Even Philip can see me wincing in pain. But his emotion doesn't change from the smile he had the moment we met.

Creepy, creepy little brat.

Emma nods and lowers the gun. It remains tight in both hands. "We're done here?" she says again. Her trust issues begin to show as she locks eyes with Asshole and takes slow steps away from him.

Asshole nods and lowers his head to the ground. "Just don't shoot."

Emma tucks the gun back into her purse and wraps her hand around Philip's shoulder. "We're going," she says. "Now."

"You don't have to ask me twice," I mutter and try to catch up.

I had nearly forgotten I was hungry by the time we get to the motel room again. My eyes strain to see, my head pulses in pain, and my hands have gone numb from the pain.

All of this lets me get into the motel room and lay down and not realize that there's a mirror right next to the television.

Philip sits down on the other bed, furthest away from the door, and bounces on it. His brown hair flops up and down over his ears with each bop.

"Philip, stop that, dear," Emma says. She comes in with a white towel, soaked with warm water. "Here," she says. She lays it on my lap. "This will help."

"With what?" I mutter. It hurts to move my fingers. I have to force myself to look at them and not feel the cold sweats and butterflies from the sight of my own blood—my own life-force—leaking out of my body. My fingers have grown three times in girth, my hands have gone from flesh-tone white to eggplant purple.

"Fuck," I mutter.

Philip laughs. "Fuck," he says and covers his mouth.

Emma shoots him a glance, but smiles when the kid isn't looking at him anymore. "That kid will be the death of me."

Like she fucking read my mind.

"Is this how you saw your story ending?" Emma says. She pulls up a chair and sits down in front of me. She leaves a healthy amount of space between us as she grips the towel gently off my lap and taps the bruises and gashes all over my hands.

"My story?"

Emma smiles and looks down as if she's embarrassed by her words. "I'm sorry, the newspaper story. You know. The one you're working on."

"Who says it's ending?"

"We don't have any more leads," she says. "Charlie isn't going to help you anymore. Not after this. You'll be lucky if he doesn't call the cops after all."

My hands tense up and I immediately wish they hadn't. Emma watches me suck back the pain but says nothing for comfort.

Bitch.

"You said he wouldn't."

"Did I?" she says. "I don't remember." Her grip on my fingers softens as she says this. But her eyes begin to look familiar. Like the smiling brat's.

And bit by bit, the wash rag turns from its soft white origins to the muddled pink, stained with dark red smears like camos from Hell's Army.

Emma dabs the last bit of blood off my fingers and then keeps the rag at a safe distance from her body, extending her arms out like my blood is nuclear waste.

"Thanks," I say.

She shrugs it off and dumps the rag in the trash. "Don't mention it."

The kid stops his bouncing and sits back against the thick wooden headboard and watches the television. It's a talk show on, someone I don't recognize. Must be local. The guest is someone who wrote a book about training pets. Dogs, I think, based on the furry thing that sits obediently next to him.

I look over at the kid and shake my head. Half of his finger is up his nose.

I get up and try to avert my eyes from the mirror in front of me. I don't feel the tingly chills that usually come with her watching me.

Those have been reserved strictly for the brat.

But to be safe, I snatch one of the thick white towels from the metal rack attached to the wall and drape it over the mirror. It's barely long enough to keep the thing covered, so it'll do until we leave tomorrow morning.

"Don't touch this," I tell Philip. I point a stern finger in his direction to show I mean business.

He doesn't look scared. Philip turns his head, then flips it my way and points a finger back at me.

"He's harmless," Emma says. "You have nothing to worry about. We won't touch it."

I let go of my muscles, my finger and hand drifts down to my side.

Maybe it was the blood loss, maybe the excitement, but my shoulders feel heavy, my eyes puffy.

"I need to sleep, I think."

For safety, I decide I'm keeping all clothes on. Emma silently acknowledges my decision with a nod and turns to face Philip, who's rubbing his stomach and whispering something to her.

The white bedsheets scratch against my pants. I'll be hot sometime in the middle of the night. I'll deal with that later.

I decide it's best to sleep on my side, tucking my arm under the pillow and facing away from the brat, toward the loud, boxy air conditioner.

"Okay, honey, I'll be right back."

Do I open my eyes? Is she leaving me here? With him?

Emma' purse jingles as it slides over her shoulder. She's careful to open the door with the least amount of sound and slips out. The cool air outside makes a suction noise that seems to seal the door shut.

I close my eyes.

There's a sound of fabric moving, bed springs shifting.

Then childish laughter as the television gets turned up.

24

JAMES

"What are you doing?"

Philip climbs onto my side of the bed and lays next to me. He crosses his arms across his abdomen and then stares up into the ceiling.

"What do you think dead people think about?" he says.

"Are you pretending you're dead?" I ask.

There's a bit of a smiling moan. "Hmmm," he moans. "Maybe. Maybe I am."

"Why?"

There's a small pause in his breathing, as he holds his breath. I should check to see if he's still breathing, but I stare up at the ceiling, trying to imagine what he's doing. Connecting dots and shadows? Making scenes in his head?

Finally, his lungs seem to release and he takes in one long gasp of breath. "No reason," he says.

There's a long pause between us and then something thuds

upstairs. Loud enough to pull me out of bed.

"What was that?"

"Probably someone falling out of bed." It's the words Philip used that caused me to watch his every move, but the way he blinked slowly, smiled, then whispered the words like it was nothing.

"Why would you say that?"

Why would you know that?

"No," Philip says. "We shouldn't call the front office and check in on them." He pauses and turns to look at me. "Unless you want to."

The pillow next to him is within reach. One snatch of the side, tossing it over his face. My teeth clench in pure adrenaline. I can already feel my muscles tense in anticipation.

He won't struggle that much. He's only nine? Ten?

I can take him.

The boy stands up, walks to the front door in steps that seem too quick for his stubby little legs. With a flick of his hand, he locks the deadbolt on the door. "Just in case," Philip says.

"In case of what?" I ask.

The boy stays by the door, but he seems to slump over a little bit as he watches the television. "In case something strange happens out there."

"That's a good idea," I mutter and rest back onto the bed. "You don't have to go stand by the door. Emma will come back soon."

Philip's nod is the only sign that he acknowledges my existence.

The room's noise begins to disappear as Philip turns down the volume.

And as I watch his face, he seems emotionless for a little boy. His lips remain still, locked in a smile with no meaning. His expressions don't change with the actions on the television.

As the two detectives follow the clues, find the killers and interview the potential suspects, the boy's emotions remain locked in at zero.

For the few minutes I watch him, he doesn't blink. He doesn't twitch. He doesn't move.

"Philip, are you hungry yet?"

He nods his head, his body shifts slightly on the bed.

The sound of the television gets punctuated with the sound of rain just outside. There's lightning slipping past the cracks in the curtains, but no sounds of cracking thunder.

And so we sit in silence of gunshots and yelling from the television.

"I'm thirsty," Philip says. He stands up, grabs a plastic cup from the bathroom counter and fills it up with water.

His movements seem smooth and fluid and calculated. Not what I'd expect a little boy's quick, excitable movements to be.

"Philip?" I say.

Leaning over the edge of the bed, watching him take a sip, there's something watching me back in the mirror.

My heart seizes, my chest clenches tight. For a moment, I forget to breathe.

The face of Mad Maddy stares me back, taking the place of where Philip would be. Her auburn hair flows loose over her shoulders and ears. Her eyes set deep into her skull.

The room in the mirror isn't like this room. No light anywhere.

Like she's coming from a world of shadows.

She smiles, but I can't see any teeth. Just blood. Thick lines creep out from the sides of her mouth, dripping down her jaw and onto Philip's head.

Then Philip looks back up at me and smiles. "What's wrong?"

"Get back from there," I mutter. My chest bubbles inside with the oncoming laughter. "Get away from there."

The air in my lungs replaces the words and my ability to leave.

"Why are you laughing?"

Philip turns around to face me. He sets the cup onto the counter and walks toward me. I see a look of concern, empty concern. He finds me on the floor.

My sides hurt, my chest grows tighter with every laugh.

"Why are you laughing?" Philip says. "Should I call Gramma?"

My eyes water from the laughter. Air won't stay in my lungs.

And behind Philip, Maddy stretches a hand out from the mirror into our reality.

Philip grabs my hand. His feet dig into the carpet and he pulls back.

My shoulder wants to go with him, but the rest of my body feels weak.

My energy gone with every laugh.

"What's your problem?" Philip says. "Get up."

"Can you?" I chuckle. "Can you see her, too?"

Philip looks back behind him, turns to look back at me. "What?"

"We have to go," I say. My body gives in to gasping convulsions. My lungs can't taste enough air for my body to swallow properly. Between chuckles and laughter, I gag and choke.

"Open the door," I say. The words are broken up, but it's clear he understands.

Philip releases my hand, letting it slap to the carpet. The cold breeze of the night air rushes in.

This is my moment. To run. To save Philip once and for all.

I can laugh, but the rest of my body wants to move. My feet scrape along the bristles of the carpet, every toe catching a little bit of traction. Enough to get me going.

But I'm too slow.

I can't look back. I can't see what just touched my toe.

Cold chills in my hips and my back. My ass muscles clench in reaction.

"Come on," I say.

It's amazing where the energy comes from when your body knows it's in trouble. I'm out the door, Philip along with me. As I'm gripping the metal railing at the edge of the walkway, Philip comes next to me and grabs my forearm with a freezing touch.

"What's wrong with you?" My knee-jerk reaction shoves the poor brat to the cement floor. He lands on his back, his elbows catching his fall. He looks at me—no, glaring at me—and seethes with anger. "What the hell?"

My laughter leaves me. I can breathe, but my chest is heavy, the air feels thin. Every little bit of muscle and tissue in my nose burns with the cold air. "We're in danger," I say. "She's here."

"Who?" Philip stands up and looks back into the window of the motel room.

I snatch him back and shield him with my arms. "No, not there. We can't go back."

"But it's cold out here."

It's true. My muscles freeze when I touch him. Philip's touch chills every part of my body down to the bone. But I can still feel the push of blood coursing through my body. Little racetracks of heat that are enough to keep me moving.

"We have to go. "

"To the car?"

"Yes," I mutter. Then, "No. Not the car. Too many windows."

Philip pushes himself out of my full grip, but his hand remains locked in mine.

What happens is less us running away together, more his feet dragging on the cement walkway, down the steps, and over the asphalt parking lot. "What?"

"I need to save you."

"I'm telling Gramma," Philip screams.

I have to bite my tongue to keep from laughing. "I can save you."

"From what?" Philip screams. His other hand grips my wrist and he pushes. His fingers feel like icicles stabbing my skin. His nails so cold they burn.

"From her," I mutter. "From your mother."

"My what?" His hands let go of my wrists and he just dangles from my arms like a ragdoll. We're nearly across the entire parking lot when his body goes damn near limp.

"Wake up," I say.

And his arm starts twitching. His legs spasm. And he looks up at me with a slight, creepy smile. "You don't need savin' from her, dummy."

My hands lock up but my arm feels weak. This gives the effect of him rollin' out from underneath my arms, but his shirt still stuck in my grip.

"What do you mean?" I ask.

Philip yanks himself free. He stands up, bent over. He checks his shoes, dusts himself off. "My momma's been dead. My dad said so."

"Your mom," I say. "I seen her. In the mirrors. In glasses. In water."

The boy starts laughing, but he calms down when he sees me shootin' him a glance.

"I seen her all around. Everywhere. I recognize her."

The boy shakes his head and stands up straight. He crosses his arms across his chest in a stance of power. Like he really thinks he'll get the upper hand here. "I saw my mom," he says. "I saw her when she was dead."

The reality of him seeing a dead body creeps in on me. And of course I do that thing that we all do when we hear something tragic—I place myself in his shoes. I imagine my own mom dead. My Maw Maw.

But all I see staring back at me in the open casket is those cold eyes of Maddy.

I shake the image from my head and turn to the boy. "You saw your momma die?"

"I didn't say that," the boy says. He looks across the street, shielding his eyes from the streetlights just a few feet from us. "I said I seen her dead."

"How? When?" I kneel down to the ground. His deep, dark eyes pierce into me. But as he speaks, describing the way his father told him, his eyes seem to soften. He frowns, his puffy cheeks growing red and blotchy.

"I'm sorry," I say.

And I am. There's not much else to say to all of that. Except sorry.

Except, it's not all that I could have said. But all I wanted to say.

My words don't seem to affect the boy one way or the other. Instead, Philip keeps his attention and his gaze onto a figure coming back across the street. It's moving quickly. Its legs are almost a blur.

"What are you staring at, anyway?"

"My grandma," Philip says.

"That can't be here," I mutter. "It can't be. She can't move that fast."

The figure grows larger and larger, finally resembling a person.

Dust kicks up around its feet. And the figure, all of it, remains a blur.

I don't know where the cold breeze came from, and why the rain started to drop only on my head and shoulders. The hair on the back of my neck and my wrists stands on end. I clench up—everywhere.

Then it shrieks into the air. The force of the scream hits me back onto my heels, but I don't fall down.

"What was that?"

The boy grabs my hand. "Just be calm," he says.

My muscles tighten up, the goosebumps on my skin grow so thick it pulls my forearms tight. And I can't move.

"It'll be over soon," the boy says.

My lungs explode with laughter. My eyes water almost instantly.

I stumble backwards. Rocks jab deep into my hands. There are more cuts, more blood leaking from the sides of my arms.

The burst of warmth along my arms is enough to keep me awake for now.

For only a moment, I can keep from laughing.

The figure moves across the street.

When I blink my eye, I can see white hair, gray face. And dark, deep, pale blue eyes.

"Emma?" I ask.

The car.

"Go," I shout.

The boy doesn't budge. His hand feels clammy in mine, but I manage to drag his stupid ass all the way to the car.

We're inside in a matter of seconds. The door slams shut. But something's missing.

"Fuck!" I let my fists pound full-force into the steering wheel.

Philip laughs in the passenger seat next to me.

"We don't have the keys."

Philip shakes his head. Says nothing.

The doors are locked. I twist all of the mirrors away from me.

But that's not enough. She can get in.

With a stray pen pointing out of the glove compartment, I jab at the little crevice between the mirror and the plastic holder. The pen's tip doesn't go in. Not deep enough.

So it's Plan B.

With the tip of the pen, I stab at the mirror, scraping and scratching at it. The thing twists up and down, weakening until it barely hangs on.

I rip the damned thing off and toss it into the backseat.

And Philip chuckles. He covers his mouth with two chubby little hands, his fingers more like Vienna sausages than useful tools.

My heart wants to rip itself out of my chest and run through the streets.

The car smells like cigarettes and the last dying cries of an air freshener. Some pine bullshit that probably smelled like a Christmas tree, but now reminds me of Christmas parties at my aunt's house.

"I can't do this," I mutter. "I can't die this way."

Philip's eyes grow wide.

I try to follow his gaze, but I can't. That would mean staring into the glasses. Looking through and into them.

No. Please no.

Everything has gotten silent.

Too silent.

My fingers itch, my palms covered with slick, hot sweat. "I can't do this. I can't."

I pop the door open and run. The cool air keeps me cold just long enough to get across the parking lot into the sharp, gray rocks that line the side of the road.

Instead of putting up a fence between this hotel and the steak house next to it, they line the area with a rocky walkway that invites people to come on over while making sure they wear shoes.

But when I want to stop, I can't.

The rocks make sure of that.

I'm sliding across the rocks, slipping and falling. My body slides just before a pile of broken glass bottles.

Green and brown.

"Shit. Shit. Shit. Shit."

I'm back on my feet, scrambling to move, but I won't.

My body won't let me.

I'm doubled over in laughter.

And in a thick, crescent-shaped shard of green beer bottle glass, an eye peers at me.

A shriek charges at me from behind.

Where is she? Why me?

I don't know where I'm going, but I move. Forward, across the rocky walkway. Forward into the second parking lot.

Forward into the steakhouse.

There's a long line to get in. Families look patiently at the decorations on the wall—photos of cowboys and bulls and rope and other cowboy shit. Dark mahogany woods line every wall in this place.

"Excuse me," I say. "I need help."

The woman at the counter takes three menus from a wooden pocket next to the podium and announces, "Johnson, party of three."

"I need help," I shout again. Everyone stares at me.

No, this isn't a game. No, I'm not trying to cut in front of you.

The silence in the room is cut by the tapping of glass and wood around me.

"No," I say. My chest heaves in fits of laughter.

An old mother grabs her young son and pulls him closer to her.

The tapping grows louder.

"Don't you hear that?" I shout. "It's her."

Everyone wearing a black polo shirt in that place stares right at me.

I know what's coming next. They think I'm a straggler. A vagrant.

"Please," I mutter. "Please help me."

These people turn their heads away from me, talking to God, ignoring me. The crowd steps to one side to let the crazy person—me—get through.

But they don't hear it. Why don't they hear it? Why am I the only one who can see her? Hear her?

I scramble across the parking lot around a chain-link fence into another parking lot. This one looks vacant on this side.

A bright sign hangs in a glass window.

VACANT.

Another hotel.

Maybe they'll help me.

But when I get to the glass doors in front, the reflections of the lights from the street flicker.

Then go dark.

My hands clasp the cold metal handles and won't let go. I know the hand is attached to me, but it doesn't want to leave the door.

The lights—the real ones, in my world—they still stay on, casting dark, midnight blue shadows on the ground.

But the ones in the mirror world burst, exploding flaming shards of glass all over the nearly empty parking lot.

A shadow slithers along the ground. Twisting and turning. Fluid like water.

I can't look away.

I want to—god dammit, I want to—but I can't.

The shadow takes a human form.

It's her. Always her.

The shape takes a curvy form, flowing with shoulder-length black hair that gradually changes color. Lighter.

I can turn my head away, but my eyes stay fixed. Magic? Mind control? Perverse curiosity? I can't look away.

The hair gets shorter, the color lighter.

Pale blue eyes stare back at me.

And the face—it's familiar.

"You?"

My shoulders spasm. My back feeling pain like I've been kicked between my shoulder blades a hundred times by a workhorse.

I have to break free.

I only have one weapon.

So I use it.

My head goes into the glass. Everything is on fire, in shades of red.

My forehead is red hot. The heat pours down to my cheeks and my chin.

I have to blink to keep my vision straight.

But there's a crack.

I can do this.

"You won't."

Slam.

"Get me."

Slam.

Everything's spinning.

But a white streak creaks across the glass like lightning in the sky. It hurts like hell, but when I press, I can make the crack bigger.

It creeps across the glass.

Until, with a punch from my other hand, the glass shatters.

And there are a million little hers. Two million eyes looking back at me.

Some of them Maddy.

Some of them Emma.

The math. The dates. The stories. Nothing added up.

Whatever held my hand to the cold metal releases me. I'm flat on my ass in a blink of an eye. But I can't move. Shards of glass stick out from my palms. Every movement feels like more glass pushes itself inside of me. Dear god, I can feel them—all of them—in my muscles.

An alarm screams from the inside of the hotel.

Someone comes to the door, but I can't see them.

All I can see are my knees, huddled up against my chest. Rocking along on my side, pushing myself up and down.

Every little piece of glass is a reflective door to her world.

To Emma. To Maddy.

"What the hell, man?" The voice is a guy. Blood blurs my vision. I can't see much beyond dark skin. Light hair.

He swears, calling me "asshole" and "fucker."

"Please," I whisper to my knees. "Help me."

I'm not sure how much time passes between me whispering to myself to someone poking me with a thick pole.

"Sir," the man says. "Sir, I'm going to have to ask you to get up."

When I can pry my eyes open, glued together from dried blood and tears, my eyes are attacked by red and blue lights swirling in the air.

"Do you know who you are?" the man says. "Do you know what day it is?"

"A Wednesday?" I ask.

The officer doesn't buy it.

"Is this the man?" the officer says. He takes a step to the side and points at a little boy. Philip. "Is this the man that took you?"

"He came with me," I mutter. "He came with."

"What's that?" The officer steps directly in front of my face. Mexican spices kick out of his mouth, ramming my nose and mouth with his breakfast burrito.

"He came with," I say. I have to shake my head to free the blocked webs of thoughts. Words. Phrases. Everything floating around my head.

"Stop shaking your head. Are you okay?"

I shake my head again. "No. Not okay, officer. She's out to get me."

"Who?" The officer pulls out something shiny from a back pocket.

"No," I say. "No cuffs."

As soon as he senses that I'm taking a step back, the officer seizes my arm. "A little help?" he says. Another smaller man grabs my other arm.

"This is gonna hurt a lil," the small guy says.

And it does. My arms get twisted around my back, my shoulders thrust forward. The cuffs are surprisingly warm. They click closed.

And Philip stands still at the edge of the cop car. His cheeks are lined with dirt, streaked with tears.

"What are you sad about?" I say. "Where's Emma?"

Philip shakes his head. "Who?" he says.

The officer takes me into another cruiser—away from Phillip. I get a warning to watch my head and he slams the door.

Look down. Away.

The officer says something onto a radio on his shoulder. Something about taking me in. Maybe an observation. Broken glass.

Property damage.

They think I'm drunk or high.

An officer climbs into the driver's seat and adjusts the mirror to talk to me. "Helluva bender last night, huh?" he says.

When my eyes meet up with his, there's a third set of eyes in the mirror smiling back at me.

25

JAMES

They say if I do what I'm told, I can get out of her sooner.

But fuck that.

I want to stay. I need to stay.

So every once in a while, I kick an orderly. I'll swear at the cafeteria ladies. Spit on someone else's food.

I can't do it all at once. If I do that, they'll double my medication. Then I sleep all day with only a few moments of clarity each day. Usually enough to barely piss in the corner and stumble back to this patchwork cot they call a bed.

Out there they have glass. Mirrors. Bottles.

In here, I have brick. Painted metal.

Not a reflective thing in sight.

A knock on the door. Little eyes peer through a slit in the thick metal door. It's painted mint green. Calming to some. It just makes me want to chew gum.

"Take your meds, goddammit."

"Yes, Calhoun," I say.

"That's Ms. Calhoun." The woman's voice makes sure I understand the Ms part of her name.

Oh, I understand all right.

I ain't misunderstood a goddamned word since I been in here.

Since they thought I was crazy.

But what I have, it's a real disease. But the lawyers couldn't spell it. The judge didn't give a shit.

I broke stuff. Stole a kid. Rambled on about a woman trying to kill me.

They said I was crazy.

I played along.

There's no safety out there.

Out there where Emma and her brat go wherever they please. Out there where they scheme against me.

I get visits every week. Emma brings me cookies.

I'm not allowed the cookies. They take everything.

Ms. Calhoun—that fat-ass—she probably takes them all. Eats them all. Tells me there were cookies to make me hate her more.

But I don't want cookies. I know what she is. I know what they all are. I know what I need. It's not cookies.

There's medicine in here. There's warmth. No responsibilities. No reflections.

The woman knocks on the door again. "I still see a full cup," she says.

My feet touch the cold floor. When the Calhoun—sorry, Ms. Calhoun—sees me up and at 'em, she eases back a bit.

After I have my fingers wrapped around the little medicine cup, pinky out, she smiles. And when they go down my throat and I stick out my tongue, she goes along her merry little way.

I'll have about a half hour before I start feeling the drowsiness. Before I'll be staring at the walls and looking for patterns and remnants of dreams I had yesterday and the day before.

Not nightmares. But dreams.

Actual fucking, goddamned dreams. Beautiful dreams or normal things like showing up to class naked. Having to give a presentation with an erection.

Normal stuff.

It's been three months since my last outburst, but the nurses and orderlies don't know I'm counting.

The lock on the door shifts and clicks. The door creaks open. Ms. Calhoun wanders in through the doorway. A large white man stands behind her. He's the hired muscle. Bald with thin gray hairs along the side of his head. A face that looks like it's seen a few fights and barely walked away from them.

Not Ms. Calhoun. She walks in like she owns my room. Her hair is brown, usually lighter than it is now. It's been a while since she's colored it. Her cheeks are what I'd call rosy and puffy. If she didn't constantly bite at her lips, she'd look like a mostly happy person.

But when she's around me, she's Mrs. Hardass.

Mostly because of stuff like this.

Back on my bed, I take my pillow and flick it at her head. It slams into her face, pushing the bun in the back of her head out of place, then plops onto the ground.

The laughing sound in the room isn't coming from me. Ms. Calhoun shoots a glance at her muscle standing at the doorway. He looks out into the hallway like he heard something suspicious.

Ms. Calhoun sighs, looks at me. "You know this means you've lost your pillow," she says sternly.

I nod. "Yes, ma'am."

David Gearing

"Why do you look so happy about that? All this misbehavior—
your choices—they're just gonna lead you back in here longer."

I nod. "I know, ma'am. I'm counting on it."

ABOUT THE AUTHOR

DAVID GEARING is the author of other New Gothic novels *Echoes, Savior, Gifted, Wannabe,* and *Mr. White.* David recently transplanted to the Pacific Northwest with his partner and lovable feline fur-child Leo.

He's an avid gamer, educator, and wanna-be rock star.

You can read Savior for free if you visit him at his publisher's website at www.akusaipublishing.com